A Hummingbird Christmas

A Hummingbird Christmas

A Glacier Creek Romance

Karen Foley

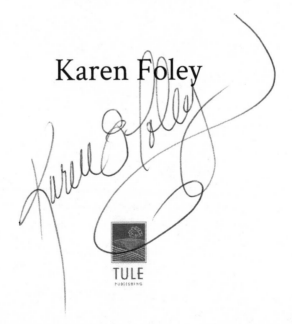

TULE
PUBLISHING

Chapter One

JOY HOLLIDAY'S KNUCKLES were white from gripping the steering wheel of the Honda CR-V she'd rented at Glacier Park International Airport just two hours earlier. What insanity had made her decide to drive to her in-laws' house tonight, instead of booking a hotel near the airport and making the drive in the morning, as she'd told them she would do?

The flight from Los Angeles had been delayed several hours due to high winds and snow in the Glacier Park region of Montana, but, by the time they'd landed, the snow had stopped coming down. The little town of Glacier Creek was only fifty miles or so south of the airport, and Joy had been sure it would be a quick, easy drive.

She glanced in the rearview mirror at her small daughter, Piper, who sat buckled into a car seat, bundled up in a brand new winter coat and hat. Beneath the hem of the coat, the tulle skirt of her pink ballet tutu frothed around her legs. She'd insisted on wearing it, and Joy given up on trying to convince her that it wasn't practical. She'd finally agreed, as long as Piper also wore a long-sleeved jersey and a pair of thick leggings beneath the insubstantial outfit.

Now the little girl stared out the car window, mesmerized by the falling snow. Joy had promised her five-year-old daughter a white Christmas, and she'd sure managed to deliver on the white part. But what had initially been beautiful, light flurries when they'd picked up the rental car had swiftly become a thick, swirling whiteout, making visibility poor, if not impossible. The lines on the road had disappeared about an hour back, and Joy drove at a snail's pace, terrified she would drive off the road.

She had no idea how much farther it was to the town of Glacier Creek, where her in-laws lived, because she was too nervous to take her hands off the steering wheel long enough to pick up her phone, which lay on the seat next to her. She hadn't passed a road sign in several miles, and gusty winds whipped off the lake to her right, billowing across the road, all but obscuring her vision.

"Are we almost there, Mommy?"

The little voice sounded anxious, and Joy recognized the warning signs of a child who desperately needed to be fed, and then tucked into bed.

"Almost, sweetie. How's your snack-pack? Have you eaten everything?"

"I don't want no more Cheerios." A note of petulance had crept into Piper's voice.

"I don't want *any* more Cheerios." Joy corrected her. "What about the apple slices? Have you eaten those?"

Piper gave a dramatic sigh, and pulled her knit hat off. Long, bright orange curls zigzagged out from her head in all directions. She plucked at the pom-pom on the top of the hat. "Yes. But I'm hot, and I have to go to the bathroom."

Joy frowned. There was no place to safely pull off the road and, even if there was, her daughter would never agree to relieve herself on the side of the road, even if the weather had allowed it.

"Just a little longer, and we'll be at Grammy and Grampy's house, and then we can have a snack and hot chocolate. Doesn't that sound good?"

Another long, dramatic sigh. "I guess so. If we ever get there."

Then Joy saw it—the road sign that indicated they had just entered the town of Glacier Creek. Thank goodness.

"We're almost there," she said, infusing her voice with cheerfulness. "Just a few more miles."

She'd studied the map so hard before they'd left the airport she'd almost memorized the directions to her in-laws' house, and knew the turnoff to their road was less than a mile from the town limits, on the left. If she reached the town center, then she'd gone too far. But with the snow coming down so fast, she couldn't see any landmarks, and she almost missed her turn. Worse, darkness had fallen and her headlights did little to penetrate the whiteout.

She turned the small SUV onto the road that led to her in-laws' house, and then reset her odometer. This was a private road, owned by the Holliday family. There was one more turn she needed to make, and it was exactly three-quarters of a mile from the main road. If she missed this next turn, the road continued into the heavily timbered foothills of the Mission Mountains, where her father-in-law owned a sawmill and lumber company.

She drove slowly up the steady incline, giving the car a little more gas in order to avoid getting stuck on the snow-covered road. Evergreen trees pressed in on both sides, heavily laden with white snow. At any other time, Joy might have found the winter scene breathtaking, but not now. She would be grateful when she made the next turn, and the large timber frame house came into view.

"Just a few more minutes," she said to her daughter. "And then we'll be able to see Grammy's Christmas tree. I'll bet Grampy strung lots of pretty lights on the house."

This made Piper sit up higher, and she strained to see out the window. "Does Grampy have a chimney? Will Santa Claus know I'm here, and not at home?"

"Grampy has a huge chimney," Joy said, smiling at her daughter in the rearview mirror. "In fact, I'll bet it's the biggest fireplace you've ever seen!"

"Mommy, look out!"

In the split-second that Joy had taken her eyes off the road, an enormous pickup truck with a plow on the front appeared, seemingly out of nowhere, directly in their path. The oncoming headlights were blinding and Joy had only an instant to react, slamming on the brakes and yanking the wheel hard to the right in order to avoid a head-on collision. The car fishtailed violently, and then they were sliding off the road as Piper screamed in terror. There was a jarring impact and the terrifying sound of crunching metal, and then it was over.

They had come to rest in a ditch, up against a tree, and

the car had pitched sideways at a steep angle so that only the seatbelt prevented Joy from sliding into the passenger seat. Frantically, she twisted around to see Piper, still strapped in her car seat, eyes wide with terror.

"Are you alright, baby?" Her voice was frantic, but the fear of something terrible happening to her child was almost paralyzing. "Are you hurt?"

Piper shook her head, mute, and Joy went weak with relief and the aftereffects of the adrenaline rush. Her headlights were still on, and the wipers still swept the falling snow from the windshield in a steady, rhythmic motion, but everything was otherwise silent.

Where the hell had that truck come from? This was a private road, owned by her in-laws, but she couldn't see her father-in-law driving in this weather. And what was she going to do now?

As if in answer to her unspoken question, there was a knock on her window, and she looked around to see a man peering through the glass at them, motioning for her to unlock her door. With the car settled almost on its side, he seemed to loom above her. The headlights from his truck were bright, and all she could make out was a dark silhouette. Knowing she didn't have much choice, she hit the unlock button.

Chapter Two

THE MAN YANKED the door open, sending a shower of cold snow down on top of Joy. She peered up at him, but all she could see were broad shoulders beneath a heavy shearling coat with the collar turned up against the snow, and a brimmed hat pulled down low. The only feature she could make out was a hard, square jaw.

"Are you okay? Is anyone injured?" The wind nearly whipped his words away.

"No," she assured him. "We're okay."

"We?" The man leaned down and stuck his head inside the car, so close that his frosted breath puffed warmly against Joy's cheek as he peered into the back seat. Seeing Piper, he recoiled, and Joy could feel him staring at her. "You're Matt Holliday's widow."

The words, hurled like an accusation, were so unexpected and so repugnant that it was her turn to recoil. For a moment, she couldn't reply.

Widow.

Was that really who she was? *Widow* was the box she checked on government forms. *Widow* was how someone described a character in a book. *Widow* was the sweet old lady from church who spent sixty-five years with the love of her life and, even then, their marriage had been cut too short.

Widow was not who she wanted to be. She was only twenty-seven years old. She didn't like to think she had now been without Matt for longer than she'd been with him.

"Yes," she finally managed to say. "How did you know?"

"Because your little girl is the spitting image of her father, that's how."

"You knew my husband?"

"Knew him? Matt was like a brother to me."

His tone held something almost like animosity, although Joy couldn't imagine why, except that maybe he was upset about the accident. He had moved to the back door of the SUV, and the headlights from his pickup truck washed over him, revealing chiseled cheekbones, and a Clint Eastwood-esque profile that could have found a lucrative career in Hollywood. His was a hard face to forget.

"You're Cole Tanner."

It was a statement, not a question. She recognized the man who had been raised alongside her late husband. Matt had looked upon this man as both a brother and a best friend. She had never met him, but Joy had seen enough photos of Cole Tanner to recognize him.

He slanted her a sideways glance. "That's right. How about we get your little girl out of here? I'll put her in my truck, where it's warm, and then come back for you."

Joy twisted around until she could see Piper, who was staring at Cole with undisguised interest. Indecision warred within her.

"Piper," she finally said. "I want you to go with Mr. Tanner. He's going to take you to his truck, and then mommy will be right there, okay?"

Piper didn't even acknowledge Joy. In an uncharacteristic display of childish trust, she was already stretching her arms out to Cole.

"Just hold on there, darlin'," he said, leaning in toward her. "Let's put your hat and mittens on first."

Joy watched as he carefully pulled Piper's hat on, and then tugged her mittens over her hands. He talked soothingly to her the entire time.

"It's cold out, and the snow is pretty deep, so I'm going to carry you to my truck. How does that sound? Good? Okay, then, here we go."

He released the harness restraint on her car seat, and before Piper had a chance to fall sideways, neatly scooped her into his arms and drew her out of the car.

Straightening, he looked at Joy. "Let me get her settled, and then I'll be right back."

Joy didn't know how to feel as she watched him stride up the snow-covered embankment with her daughter in his arms. She knew he and her husband had grown up together, but did she really know anything about him? What if he tried to drive off with her little girl? Unbuckling her seat belt, she grabbed hold of the door frame and tried to climb out of the driver's seat, but had misjudged the steep angle of the car, and nearly fell backwards into the passenger side.

She'd removed her coat and hat earlier, and saw they had

slid from the passenger seat onto the floor, beyond her reach. Now the whipping snow stung at her face and the cold snatched her breath away as she tried to pull herself forward and out of the car.

"Hey, let me help you," Cole called, as he made his way back toward her.

"Is Piper okay?"

"She's fine. I'm going to take you to the truck, and then I'll come back for her car seat and your belongings." He took a moment to brace his feet, and then leaned in toward her, balancing one gloved hand on the doorframe. "Put your arms around my neck. I'll pull you up."

Joy did as he asked and wrapped her arms around his broad shoulders, feeling the cold snow that covered his coat seep through the material of her shirt. He put his free arm around her, and pulled her out of the car, until her feet made contact with the ground.

"Okay, I'm good," she said, trying to ignore the bitter wind that cut through her like a knife. "I can walk."

But before she could pull away from Cole, he lifted her in his arms as easily as if she weighed no more than Piper, and carried her up to the road, where his truck sat idling. Only when he'd reached the cab did he finally set her down.

"Th-thank you," she managed. She couldn't prevent her teeth from chattering.

"Here," Cole said, and began unbuttoning his coat. "You're freezing. Take this."

"No, I'm f-fine."

But he'd already settled the heavy coat around her shoulders. He opened the door to the truck and helped her into the cab with one strong hand under her elbow, and then closed the door behind her. Piper sat in the center of the bench seat, with a seat belt secured around her waist, and a smart phone in her hands. Heat blasted from the dashboard vents.

"Oh, sweetie!" Joy grabbed her daughter in a grateful embrace, ignoring the child's muffled protests. "Are you sure you're okay?"

"Mommy, I can't breathe!"

Joy kissed Piper's soft cheek and then released her. Cole's jacket still held his body's warmth, and a woodsy, masculine scent lingered in the fabric. She slid her arms inside the coat sleeves, which came down below her fingertips, and drew the front closed around her body. Tucking her chin into the shearling lining, she breathed deeply. How long had it been since she'd inhaled the scent of a man? The weight and warmth of the heavy jacket was comforting. Grateful she and Piper were both safe, she leaned over to see what had captured the child's attention on the smart phone.

"What are you doing?"

"It's a game," Piper replied, her gaze fixated on the screen, where tiny birds were used as projectiles to destroy what looked like a fortress of pigs. "Mr. Tanner showed me how to do it."

He returned then, materializing through the snow to place Piper's car seat and their suitcases into the bed of the truck. Then he opened the driver's door and shook off the snow, before climbing behind the wheel. He handed Joy her coat and hat, and the oversized tote bag that contained her pocketbook and the myriad essentials she'd packed for the plane and car ride.

Joy peeked inside, looking for the small box that she'd carefully packed and carried onto the plane. The box contained something very special, and she would be devastated if anything should happen to what lay inside. But the box was there, and Joy gave a small sigh of relief.

"What about the rental car?" she asked.

"I'll call for a tow truck in the morning, once the storm passes." Cole thrust the truck into gear, and carefully reversed on the snowy road, turning back in the direction that Joy had originally been traveling. "Why don't you buckle up?"

"Do we have far to go?" She pulled the seatbelt across her waist, and put her arm around Piper, hugging the little girl against her as the truck slowly began to move.

"Not far. I was just leaving Eldon and Beth's house when I ran into you." He kept his eyes on the road, and didn't so much as crack a smile. "No pun intended."

Joy watched Cole covertly as he maneuvered the truck through the snow. With his brimmed hat and heavy flannel shirt, he looked like the quintessential Montana cowboy, but she knew better. Cole Tanner was a smokejumper, part of the Glacier Creek wildfire crew. He'd trained with her husband, Matt. *Late* husband, she reminded herself.

Her throat tightened, as it always did when she thought of Matt. He'd been gone for almost four years and, while time had managed to soften the pain of his loss, thinking about him was like pressing on a bruise. Matt and Cole had been part of the same smoke jumping crew until six years ago, when she and Matt had met at a party in Santa Barbara. He'd been part of a larger group of hot shot teams and smokejumpers from around the country, battling a wildfire in the Los Padres National Forest. After the fire had been contained, a group of the firefighters had been invited to the same beach house where she'd been staying with friends. Their attraction had been immediate and mutual, and they'd been married less than three months later.

"How long since you've been back to Montana?"

Cole's question pulled Joy out of her thoughts. They were turning onto the road that led to the Holliday house, and Joy could see why they'd almost collided. He'd been pulling out of the road, but the dense forest, combined with the wintry conditions had made it nearly impossible for him to see her car until the last minute. They were lucky the accident hadn't been worse.

"I haven't been back since Piper was a baby," Joy admitted. "There never seemed to be a good time, and Eldon and Beth always seemed happy to come visit us in California."

"So they only see their granddaughter once a year?"

There it was again, the underlying hostility, and this time Joy was certain she wasn't imagining it.

"They come out to California and stay with us every year for her birthday in June, and again at Christmas." She kept her voice low, but knew she sounded defensive. "They said they preferred to come to us, because they didn't want me traveling alone with a young child."

"So why now?"

Joy glanced at Piper. How to explain to this man that her daughter had asked Santa for just three things this year?

A white Christmas, a puppy, and a new daddy.

She didn't want Piper to know that she'd opened the letter the little girl had written to Santa Claus. She had entrusted the letter to Joy, who had promised to mail it to the North Pole. Even now, the letter was tucked away inside her pocketbook.

She couldn't show Piper's Christmas list to anyone, not even to Eldon or Beth. While the little girl's request for a new daddy was completely understandable, Matt's parents might not understand. They would feel hurt. Piper had no memory of her father, who had died while fighting a wildfire when Piper was barely two years old. Joy hoped that by bringing her to Glacier Creek, Piper would have the white Christmas she was dreaming of, and also feel closer to the daddy she never knew. The puppy would have to wait, at least until they had a bigger place to live. Now she looked at Cole and considered how to answer his question without giving away Piper's secret.

"I thought it would be a nice change for her grandparents to have us come here, and Piper has never seen snow before," she said. "It's a nice change for us, too."

"They aren't expecting you until tomorrow," he replied, and his gloved hands flexed around the steering wheel.

"Is that a problem?" She glanced at Piper, but the little girl was too absorbed in her game to pay them any attention.

Cole glanced at her. "Knowing Beth, she's had your

rooms ready and the pantry stocked for at least two weeks. No, I can't think arriving a day early will be a problem, but they'll be surprised."

That had been the point, but Joy didn't say so to the taciturn man sitting on the far side of the cab. He didn't look like the kind of guy who particularly liked surprises.

When they rounded a bend in the road and the commanding home, with its stunning prow-front and soaring stone chimney, came into view, Joy frowned. Maybe she should have called her in-laws to let them know they were arriving early. With the exception of a small light over the recessed entry, the sprawling mountain house was almost completely dark. There was a light on in an upstairs window, but that was all.

"Are they even home?" she wondered aloud.

Cole pulled as close to the entry as he could, and killed the engine. "I just plowed their driveway, not fifteen minutes ago. Beth tends to work on her quilting in one of the spare bedrooms, and Eldon is probably in his office on the lower level of the house."

Piper lifted her head and peered out the window. "Are we here?"

"We sure are, pipsqueak," Cole answered.

Piper frowned. "Where are all the Christmas lights, Mommy? You said Grampy would have pretty lights on the house."

"Maybe he just turned them off for the night," Joy said. "Why don't we ask him?"

"I don't want to go in." Piper drew closer to Joy's side.

"It looks scary."

Cole turned his attention to the little girl, his expression one of exaggerated surprise. "Scary? Are you serious?" He leaned down and lowered his voice conspiratorially. "I happen to know that inside that house is the biggest batch of homemade chocolate chip cookies you've ever seen. Your grandma just finished baking them tonight, and she wouldn't let me have one because she said they were for *you*." He punctuated the word with a light touch of his gloved finger to the end of Piper's nose. "How does that sound?"

Piper laughed, revealing the gap where she'd recently lost her two front teeth. "Good!"

"Good. Then let's go inside and see if we can rustle up some hot cocoa to go with those cookies. Then, you can sleep snug as a bug in your own bunk bed."

Piper sucked in an excited breath and snapped her attention to Joy, her expression one of hopeful excitement. "Can I, Mommy? Can I sleep in a bunk bed?"

"We'll see," Joy hedged, casting a swift look at Cole.

She wasn't sure she appreciated his assumption that Piper would sleep in a bunk. She was only five, after all. More confusing was his easy use of the nickname that only Matt had ever used for Piper.

Shaking off her unease, she reached for the door handle. "Well, let's go in and see if anyone is still up."

Joy climbed down from the truck. The snow was still coming down fast. Slinging her tote bag over one shoulder, she turned to help Piper down, but Cole was there before her, reaching in to undo the little girl's seatbelt and lift her out, settling her easily on his hip. He gestured toward the door.

"Best get inside before we catch pneumonia."

Realizing she still wore Cole's heavy coat, and that he had nothing but a flannel shirt to protect him from the elements, Joy hurried to the door. Before she reached it, however, a lamp post at the end of the walkway came on, flooding the driveway and walkway with bright light, and illuminating the falling snow. The heavy door opened, and Joy's mother-in-law, Beth, stood in the entrance, her face registering both astonishment and happiness.

A slim, elegant woman in her mid-sixties, her red hair had long since turned to silver, and she wore it in a chin-length bob. Joy couldn't recall a time when the older woman hadn't looked completely pulled together. Even tonight, she wore a billowy white blouse over a pair of black slacks, and silver hoops dangled from her ears. She didn't look like she could possibly be a grandmother, despite the fact she insisted that both Piper and Joy call her Grammy.

"Oh, my heavens, what a surprise!" She stepped back to allow Joy and Cole to pass, but not without stealing a kiss from both Piper and Joy as they stepped through the door. "My little girl is getting so big! What a pretty pink skirt you're wearing!" She looked at Joy. "Why didn't you call? I wasn't expecting you until tomorrow! You shouldn't have driven down in this weather, and however did you run into Cole?"

"*Run into* is about the size of it," Cole said, as Beth closed the door behind them. "I was turning onto the mountain road and nearly collided with her car coming up the hill."

Beth led them into an enormous family room, flipping lights on as she went. "Where is your car now?" she asked, looking at Joy.

"In a ditch," Joy replied, brushing the snow from her hair.

Beth gasped and reached for Piper, taking the child from Cole's arms. "Well, thank goodness you're all safe."

She kissed Piper's face before setting the child on her feet, and unzipping her coat. Piper pulled her hat off, releasing her springy red hair, and Beth made a strangled sound. She took Piper's coat and hat and quickly turned away, but not before Joy saw the sheen of tears in the older woman's eyes.

"I'll just go hang these up, and then heat some milk for hot chocolate," she said over her shoulder. Without looking at them, she disappeared into the kitchen.

Joy frowned. "Is she okay?"

Cole glanced at Piper, who was staring around her in awe. He kept his voice low. "Like I said, your little girl looks just like her daddy."

He had removed his brimmed hat and, for the first time, Joy got a good look at him. His hair was thick and brown, with brighter hints of gold in it. He looked older than his twenty-nine years, with laugh lines at the corners of his eyes, and a shadow of beard growth on his square jaw that did nothing to detract from his good looks. He was tall, over six feet, with broad shoulders and lean hips, and long legs clad in denim.

When he gave her a quizzical look, she realized she was staring at him, and quickly dragged her gaze away, feeling her cheeks go warm.

"Your coat," she said, suddenly flustered. She shrugged the shearling jacket off, and handed it to him. "Thank you for everything you've done."

"Well, considering it was partly my fault, it was the least I could do."

Joy glanced in the direction of the kitchen, where Beth had disappeared. "Are you sure she's okay?"

Cole looked down at the coat he held in his hands, and his fingers tightened around the hide. When he looked back at Joy, there was a sadness in his expression that caught at her heart.

"She'll be okay. I think it's just seeing—"

Before he could finish, a booming voice interrupted them. "Where's my granddaughter?"

"Grampy!"

Joy turned to see her father-in-law, Eldon, enter the room. He was a big man with snow white hair and craggy features that creased into a smile as Piper flung herself into his arms. He lifted the little girl high in the air, and Piper squealed in delight.

"You've grown," he declared gruffly, and set her down, ruffling her hair. "I can hardly lift you anymore!"

"Again!" Piper demanded, stretching her arms up. "Make me fly!"

"Piper," Joy admonished lightly, "Grampy's right. You're

too big for him to pick up."

"Hello, darlin'," Eldon said, smiling at Joy.

She allowed herself to be enfolded in his bearlike embrace, breathing in the scent of wool and pipe tobacco that she always associated with him.

"Hello, Eldon," she said, and kissed his weathered cheek.

"I didn't think you were coming until tomorrow morning. How was your trip?"

"Well…" Joy looked at Cole. "It was mostly uneventful."

"We crashed into a tree!" Piper exclaimed dramatically. "Mr. Tanner rescued us."

Eldon's face clouded. "Where was this?"

"At the turnoff to the mountain road," Cole said. "We left the rental car there, and I'll call a tow truck in the morning to have it hauled out of the ditch."

"You should have waited until morning," Eldon told Joy in a rough voice, "instead of risking your life—and my granddaughter's—by driving in these conditions. That was foolhardy."

Taken aback by the unexpected censure, Joy watched as Eldon walked over to the stacked stone fireplace that rose through the center of the room and up through the cathedral ceiling. He stoked the banked coals until sparks began to fly, and then threw several logs on top.

He had changed.

In the six months since Joy had last seen Eldon, he'd aged. He had always struck her as a virile older man, but now he just seemed old. Feeling unaccountably stricken, Joy blinked back sudden tears and looked away. She focused instead on the beautiful room, that she'd only seen once before, when Piper was a baby.

The mountain home had a prow front with soaring windows that drew the eye upward to the rustic timber trusses overhead, joined with wooden pegs. An oversized sofa and two leather club chairs formed a cozy sitting area in front of the fireplace. Beth had a flair for design, and the rough timbers were balanced by the bright red and turquoise accents of the rugs and pillows, and the contemporary artwork on the walls. While the room had a rustic elegance, something was missing. Joy was still trying to control her emotions, when her daughter interrupted her thoughts.

"Grampy," Piper chirped, climbing into one of the leather chairs, "where is your Christmas tree? Mommy said you would have pretty lights on the house, but you don't. Why?"

Joy turned to see how Eldon would respond, but he was slow in turning from where he still poked at the fire. Joy realized that Piper had exactly voiced what was lacking in the house. Christmas was little more than a week away, and yet there were no Christmas decorations of any kind, anywhere. There was no holiday greenery, no ornaments, and no wrapped gifts. It was as if Eldon and Beth had no intention of acknowledging the holiday season at all.

As she watched Eldon, something else struck Joy that was infinitely sadder than not having a Christmas tree. There were no pictures of Matt or Piper anywhere. Joy distinctly remembered that the mantle had once displayed a half dozen or more photos of Matt, alongside pictures of baby Piper. Joy sent new pictures of Piper to her in-laws about every three months. There should have been a dozen photos on display. Instead, there were just two candlesticks on the hand-hewn, log mantle.

Eldon had not yet responded to Piper's question about the Christmas tree, and the silence in the room seemed deafening. Joy bent over Piper's chair and kissed the top of her curly head.

"There's still lots of time to decorate, sweetheart." She glanced at Cole, but he had pulled his coat on, and was turning his hat in his hands and not looking at anyone. He seemed anxious to leave. "I think Grammy and Grampy were just waiting for you to arrive so that you could help them with all the decorations," Joy said. "Did you know that in some countries, they don't put up their tree until Christmas Eve?"

Piper looked up at her with wide, trusting eyes. "Is that what we're going to do?"

Eldon was still making a show of tending the fire, so Joy gave her daughter a reassuring smile. "I promise you there will be a Christmas tree before Santa comes."

Eldon turned around and, for an instant, Joy saw raw grief reflected in his eyes. Matt had been their only child, and she understood what they felt. He had been her husband, after all, and she had loved him, too.

"How about some hot cocoa and chocolate chip cookies?" Beth's voice was falsely cheerful, as she entered the room carrying a tray laden with mugs and a heaping plate of cookies. She placed it on the low, wide coffee table in front of the fireplace, and motioned for Piper to come sit on the floor near the table.

As Joy watched her add whipped cream to Piper's hot chocolate, Cole came to stand by her side. Eldon had retreated to the windows on the opposite side of the room, and now he stood staring silently into the darkness of the surrounding night.

"Don't expect too much in the way of holiday festivities," Cole said quietly in her ear, too low for anyone else to hear. "They haven't been much for celebrating Christmas since—"

He broke off.

Since Matt died.

Joy stared at Cole in disbelief. "But they always seem so happy when they spend Christmas with us in California."

"Maybe that's just what they want you to see," he replied. "I think it's harder for them here, where their memories of Matt are strongest."

Joy didn't know what to say. She'd been devastated when Matt had died, but she'd managed to pick up the pieces and move on with her life for the sake of their daughter. Had there been moments when grief had threatened to swamp her? Of course. But she'd had a toddler who desperately needed her, so she had tried to do more than just go through the motions. She understood the sorrow that her in-laws must still be feeling, but to not celebrate Christmas was unthinkable, especially when they knew their little granddaughter still believed in Santa Claus.

"Matt wouldn't want them to be so sad," she murmured. "He would want them to celebrate his life, not continue to grieve his death."

Cole looked at her, his expression shuttered. "All I'm saying is be mindful that not everyone is ready to celebrate Christmas joy."

Without waiting for a reply, he jammed his hat onto his head, and called out a terse farewell to Eldon and Beth. Piper looked up and gave him a big smile, a chocolate moustache rimming her upper lip.

"Bye, Mr. Tanner!"

"Bye, pipsqueak. I'll see you again soon."

Joy watched him leave, his words replaying themselves in her head. *Not everyone is ready to celebrate Christmas joy.* Did he speak only for her in-laws, or also for himself?

Piper blew on her hot chocolate, sending sprays of whipped cream over the rim of the mug. She laughed in delight, and gave her grandmother a happy grin.

Joy knew her daughter had high expectations for this Christmas holiday. If what Cole said was true, then Joy had arrived in the nick of time.

Chapter Three

THE FOLLOWING MORNING dawned clear and sunny and, from where she sat on the edge of the enormous, rustic bed in the guest bedroom, Joy could see all the way to Flathead Lake. The world was blanketed in glittering white, and the sun was so bright she had to squint to look out the window. She'd never seen anything as beautiful as the towering pine trees covered in snow, or the distant mountain peaks.

From downstairs, she could hear Piper's voice, and a deeper voice responding. Lifting her nose, she breathed in the aromas of freshly brewed coffee and sizzling bacon. She slid her feet into her slippers and pulled a warm, flannel bathrobe on over her shorts and tee shirt, and made her way downstairs.

The second floor had a balcony that overlooked the great room, and Eldon had already built a fire in the enormous fireplace. As she approached the kitchen, she heard Piper laughing uncontrollably, the way only a five year old could.

"Someone is being silly this morning," Joy commented, as she entered the room, and then stopped abruptly.

Cole sat at the kitchen table across from Piper. With his

chair pushed back, his long legs extended, and a steaming cup of coffee in one hand, he looked completely at home. He was grinning at Piper, who was eating a bowl of cereal. She held her spoon midair as she laughed so hard that milk came out of her nose.

Cole gave a shout of surprised laughter and leaped to his feet, reaching for a kitchen towel. But Joy was already there, snatching up a napkin and pressing it to Piper's face as the child's laughter turned into a coughing fit, and her eyes began to stream.

"Okay, let's settle down and finish your breakfast," Joy admonished gently, when Piper could finally talk.

She couldn't bring herself to look at Cole, and only hoped she didn't look like a complete wreck. She resisted the urge to smooth her hair. She hadn't even glanced into a mirror before coming downstairs, and could only imagine how she must appear.

"Mommy, did you see that?" Piper exclaimed. "Milk came out my *nose!*"

"I did see that," Joy said, suppressing a smile. "What made you laugh so hard, anyway?"

"Cole was telling me a funny story about when he and Daddy were little," she said, and gave another laugh for emphasis. "It was so funny!"

Now Joy did look at him. He bent his head to his coffee, but a smile still lingered and, for a moment, Joy found herself transfixed by the way it changed his face. There was no denying the man was hands-down attractive, but when he smiled...

Joy looked quickly away.

The table had been set, and a large glass pitcher of orange juice stood next to a basket filled with what looked like homemade blueberry muffins, thickly crusted with a sugar topping. Joy pretended interest in those, instead.

"Something smells divine," she said.

"Good morning," Beth said from where she stood at the big, red-enameled cook stove. She wore a bright red apron over a wool sweater and jeans, and managed to look both elegant and casual at the same time. She indicated the muffins. "Cole brought those over from the Ginger Snap Bakery, and I've just made pancakes and bacon. How would you like your eggs?"

Joy turned to her mother-in-law. "I'll eat whatever is easy. Is everyone having breakfast? Where's Grampy?"

"He already ate," Piper offered.

"He's working on a new home design for a client," Beth said, deftly cracking two eggs onto a griddle. "He wants to have the plans finished before Christmas."

"Ah. I understand."

Eldon owned a lumber company, but he was also the sole proprietor of Holliday Homes, a timber frame company that designed and built luxury homes for clients all over the country, using wood that had been harvested and milled right in Glacier Creek. Their mountain home was one of their premier designs, and Eldon had an office on the lower level of the house, where he worked on house plans and met with clients. Joy recalled that Matt had hoped to build a timber frame vacation home for them one day. They had planned to spend their holidays in Glacier Creek.

Pushing the thought aside, Joy retrieved a mug from the cupboard and poured herself some coffee. The kitchen was as impressive as the great room, with a fireplace at one end, and a wall of French doors at the other end that opened onto an enormous outdoor deck, buried now beneath a foot or more of snow. Overhead, wooden trusses spanned the cathedral ceiling, and polished granite surfaces covered the cook's island and countertops, while the cabinetry had been painted a deep, dark green. Privately, Joy thought the house was a perfect place to showcase the Christmas season, and she could easily imagine the stone fireplaces draped in greenery. If it was up to her, she would have a tree in each room, sparkling with vintage, glass ornaments.

"Mommy, can we go to the festibul?" Piper asked, pulling Joy out of her musings.

At Joy's questioning look, Cole shrugged. "She means the annual Glacier Creek Christmas Festival," he explained. "It takes place downtown—well, all over town, really. The opening ceremonies are today, and the festival runs through Christmas Eve day. There's an arts and crafts fair, food tents, sleigh rides, and all sorts of activities for the kids." He gave Piper a meaningful look. "I even heard a rumor that Santa Claus himself might be there."

Piper gave a small gasp of excitement and looked at Joy. "Can we go, Mommy? Please?"

"Absolutely," she said, smiling at her daughter. "We'll ask Grampy if we can borrow his truck."

"That reminds me; I had your car towed to a garage this

morning," Cole said. "There's some damage to the front quarter panel."

"Oh. Thank you." Joy pulled out a chair next to Piper and sat down. "I'll call the rental agency and see if they can bring out a new car."

"No need," Cole said. "Between Eldon, Beth, and myself, there are four vehicles available, and you're welcome to use any of them. Or," he added casually, "I could just drive you."

"I would feel better if you let Cole take you into town," Beth said. "The roads can be tricky with the snow, and parking is limited. But Cole can always park at the firehouse, and it's an easy walk from there."

"You're still with the forest service?" Joy asked, sipping her coffee.

"Yes, ma'am. Right now it's the off-season, so I'm happy to take you and Piper into town."

The French doors to the deck were directly behind Cole, casting him in a halo of bright sunlight. He wore a dark blue chamois shirt with the cuffs rolled back over his strong wrists. He cradled his coffee between his hands, and Joy couldn't help but notice how big and capable they looked, with long, tapered fingers and neat nails. He wore no rings.

"I wouldn't want to put you to any trouble," Joy demurred. When she pulled her gaze up to his, she realized his eyes were almost as blue as the shirt he wore.

"It's no trouble."

"Here we are," Beth said, and placed a large platter of pancakes, eggs, and bacon on the table between Cole and

Joy. She paused in the act of pulling out a chair, her gaze riveted on something behind Cole, through the French doors.

Following her gaze, Joy realized there were several bird feeders mounted on the far railing of the outside deck. A quick movement caught her eye, and she half rose from her chair in disbelief.

"Is that—"

"A hummingbird," Beth confirmed, her face expressing wonder.

Joy stood up, aware Cole had turned in his chair to see what had captured their attention. Walking carefully around the end of the table, she stood by the French doors and stared at the tiny hummingbird that flitted between the feeders. It flashed iridescent green and red in the sunlight, its tiny wings beating faster than she could see as it hovered over the snow.

"A hummingbird in winter." She breathed in awe. She turned and looked at Beth. "How is that possible?"

"There is a species that overwinters in Montana," Beth said, "but this is the first time I've seen one. I'll put out some nectar, although it will likely freeze in these temperatures."

"Mommy sees hummingbirds all the time," Piper announced. "She says that Daddy sends them from heaven."

"What's this?" Cole asked, his gaze sharpening on Joy.

She watched the tiny bird as it hovered on the deck, and then finally flitted away. Returning to her chair, she helped herself to a pancake and two eggs, before handing several strips of bacon to Piper.

"Matt believed that hummingbirds were messengers from heaven," she finally said, smiling at Piper. "He said that when you see one, you have to pay close attention because someone is trying to send you a message."

"Someone who has passed?" Cole asked carefully.

Joy could hear the skepticism in his voice. "Yes."

"Mommy sees hummingbirds *everywhere*," Piper explained, stretching her arms wide, as if to demonstrate the magnitude of the phenomenon.

"So what messages are they bringing?" Cole asked. He sat back in his chair, his gaze riveted on Joy. While not quite challenging, his tone wasn't exactly one of friendly interest.

"I don't know," Joy admitted. She shrugged. "Maybe it's nothing more than coincidence, but I do see a lot of hummingbirds."

"That's not so surprising. They're fairly common, especially in the warmer climates like California."

"Well, it's hardly warm here in Montana," she said, feeling a need to defend herself, "and yet you saw it—a hummingbird in the middle of winter."

"I think it's a lovely story," Beth said, preventing Cole from answering. She had retrieved a field book of birds from a nearby shelf and was thumbing through the pages. "The one you just saw is a called an Anna's Hummingbird. They're one of the few kinds that don't always migrate south for the winter."

"Anna's hummingbird?" Piper pulled a face. "They should be called Joy's hummingbirds, because that's my mommy's name."

The conversation turned to other things, including the Christmas festival, and when they might actually drive into town. Joy ate her breakfast, but she hardly tasted her food, acutely aware of Cole's scrutiny. It didn't matter if he believed the story about hummingbirds, or not. The important thing was that Matt had believed it, and so did she.

But that led to another thought. If the hummingbird they saw outside the window really was a little messenger, what was it trying to tell her?

Chapter Four

COLE TOLD HIMSELF he'd only come over to the house for breakfast to please Beth, and not because he'd wanted to see Joy Holliday again. But there'd been no denying the way his pulse reacted the moment she'd walked into the kitchen. The only other time he'd felt that swift surge of anticipation was just before he flung himself out of a jump plane in preparation for battling a wildfire. He'd never thought he could feel the same rush just from seeing a woman.

With her bed-tousled hair and her face still softly bleary with sleep, she'd been infinitely appealing. He couldn't help but wonder if she looked that way after sex. In the next instant, he'd been full of self-loathing for allowing his thoughts to even stray in that direction. Joy was Matt's widow, and Matt had been Cole's closest friend, ever since he had arrived in the small town of Glacier Creek at the age of eight. They'd been best buds and coconspirators in everything, practically from the moment they'd first met at the Holliday sawmill, where Cole's father had gotten a job as a seasonal worker.

Cole had excused himself from the table immediately

after breakfast, on the pretext of checking the fire. Now he stood in front of the soaring windows of the great room, staring with unseeing eyes at the snow-covered mountains and the frozen tundra of Flathead Lake, wishing he hadn't come over for breakfast. He didn't want to find Matt's widow so attractive. So damned sexy.

From the kitchen, he could hear the sounds of dishes clattering, punctuated by female laughter and Piper's childish voice. He could understand now why Matt had fallen so hard and so fast for Joy.

But he still couldn't understand why Joy had kept Matt away from Montana while he had been alive. Matt had loved Montana. He'd loved the town of Glacier Creek, and he'd loved his job as a wildland firefighter. But he'd given all that up to live in Santa Barbara with Joy. He'd given up smoke jumping, and had taken a job as a hot shot with the California team, but Cole couldn't help but wonder if Matt might still be alive if he'd remained in Montana.

It was unfair of him to blame Joy for Matt's death, but she hadn't been there to see how devastating his loss had been for Eldon and Beth. Part of his anger was his own guilt. He hadn't attended their wedding because he'd been in Alaska, battling a wildfire near the Yukon Territory. When they had brought their infant daughter to Montana, it had been during the height of the wildfire season. Cole had been fighting a blaze on the eastern side of Glacier National Park and had missed their visit. He could have traveled to California to visit them, afterwards, but he hadn't.

And then it had been too late.

He wanted to dislike Joy; to put the blame for Matt's death squarely on her, but he couldn't. Part of him knew that if he had met Joy first, he might have done the same thing Matt had done—he might have given up everything just to have her in his life.

"You okay, son?"

Eldon came to stand beside him at the windows. For as far back as Cole could recall, this man had called him *son*. Not because he actually thought of him as a son, but because he called all men who were twenty years his junior by that nickname. But Cole liked to think that maybe, on some level, Eldon did think of Cole like a son. He'd certainly treated him like a son, taking him into his home the year that Cole's drifter father had vanished on Christmas Eve, leaving his eight-year-old child alone in the world.

"I'm okay," he replied.

From the kitchen, Piper laughed at something, and the sound carried through the house like the tinkling of tiny bells.

"Nice to hear a child's laughter in this house again," Eldon said gruffly.

Cole raised his eyebrows in surprise, but didn't respond beyond a nod of acknowledgment. Eldon was by nature a reticent man, and he never talked about his feelings.

"Grampy!"

Both men turned to see Piper and Joy enter the room. Piper ran to her grandfather and hugged him around his leg, while he held his coffee away in order not to accidentally spill it on her.

"Hello, darlin'," he said, stroking her springy curls. "How was your breakfast?"

"Good! Grampy, when can we get a Christmas tree? To-day?"

Someone else might have missed the pained expression that flashed across Eldon's face, but Cole didn't. Christmas had always been a big deal at the Holliday house, but that had been before Matt died. Since his death, neither Eldon nor Beth had seemed interested in celebrating Christmas in Montana. Instead, they flew to California and spent the holiday with Joy and Piper and, during their absence, the mountain house remained closed up and dark.

Now Eldon looked at the little girl and Cole could see his smile was forced. "How can I refuse?"

Piper jumped up and down with excitement. "Today? Right now?"

"Piper," Joy chided lightly, and smiled apologetically at the two men. "Why don't we go get dressed, and then we can decide about a tree later."

Cole knew the last thing Eldon wanted to do was shop for a tree. That had always been Matt's job, and he'd always brought home the biggest spruce he could find. He and Cole would set it up in front of the windows, and Beth would laughingly complain that she didn't have enough lights or ornaments to do justice to such an enormous tree. But she always did, and the tree was always magnificent.

"I have another idea for what we can do today," he said, crouching in front of the child. "I have a dog named Lucy, and she recently had pups. They're getting pretty big, and I

35

think poor Lucy is tired from having to take care of them all. How would you like to come to my house and play with them, so that Lucy can take a nap?"

Cole watched as Piper's eyes grew round and a smile spread across her freckled face. She turned to look up at Joy. "Can I, Mommy?"

Cole didn't miss how Joy looked at Eldon for approval, and only when the older man gave a barely perceptible nod, did she agree.

"Okay, but only for a little while. We don't want Mr. Tanner to think he has to entertain us," she said, sliding a quick glance in his direction.

"You'd be doing me a favor," he assured her. "The pups are about nine weeks old, and they need the socialization."

"How many puppies do you have?" Piper asked.

"There are six of them," Cole said, rising to his feet.

Piper drew in an awed breath. "Six puppies!"

"Let's go get dressed, and then we can go see them," Joy said, gently steering her daughter in the direction of the staircase. She looked at Cole. "Give us about thirty minutes? I'd like to take a quick shower."

"Take as much time as you need."

As they climbed the staircase, Joy lifted the hem of her bathrobe out of the way, and Cole had a glimpse of slim, tanned calves. He looked quickly away.

When they returned about forty minutes later, Joy had pulled her wavy brown hair back into a ponytail. Small silver disks dangled from each earlobe, catching the light and drawing his attention to her face. She wore a winter-white turtleneck sweater over a pair of snug jeans, and Cole tried not to notice how they hugged the curve of her hips and thighs.

Piper, dressed in a bright red tutu over green corduroys and a flowered sweater, with her unruly hair tamed into a single braid, ran through the house in search of her grandmother, her red skirts billowing around her.

"Grammy, where's my coat? We're going to see Mr. Tanner's puppies!"

"She has unusual taste in fashion," Cole said, slanting an amused look toward Joy.

Joy shrugged and smiled. "I took her to see a performance of the Nutcracker ballet about three weeks ago. Now she's obsessed with becoming a ballerina. I find it's easier to just let her wear what she wants. I hope this isn't an imposition for you."

"I wouldn't have suggested it if it was," he said.

"Do you live far?"

"About a mile from here. I bought ten acres of land from Eldon about five years ago, and built a house. It's just down the mountain road."

Joy was silent, and when Cole looked at her, saw her expression was pensive. Matt had also purchased land from Eldon, and his plan had been to build a vacation home where he could bring his family during the off-season. But he'd never had the chance to get started on the project. Had Joy known about the property? Was she thinking about that right now?

"C'mon, Mommy!" Piper stood impatiently in the

doorway, already bundled into her coat and hat, while Grammy tried to pull her mittens on.

In an instant, Joy's expression changed and she smiled at her daughter. "Okay, Miss Bossy! We're coming!"

The drive to his house took about five minutes, but Cole was acutely conscious of Joy sitting on the far side of cab, looking pretty in a white wool coat, which complemented her sweater, and a red knit hat over her glossy hair. As they passed the spot where her car had gone off the road, he saw her look at the tree, and the telltale mark where the tree bark had been sheared off. She gave a barely perceptible shudder, and her arm went around Piper, squeezing the little girl.

Cole could well imagine the burden she must feel, being a single parent. He could almost read her thoughts. If anything happened to her, Piper would be left an orphan. He gripped the steering wheel, thinking of his own childhood. He hadn't been too much older than Piper when his own father had abandoned him, essentially leaving him an orphan. If it hadn't been for Beth and Eldon taking him in, who knew what would have happened to him? He likely would have gone into foster care.

Slowing the truck, he turned down a narrow, snow-packed road, with pine trees on either side that bowed overhead from the weight of the snow on their branches. Sunlight filtered through, making the tree limbs sparkle.

"Oh, how pretty!" Joy breathed, peering upwards through the windshield.

A gust of wind caught one of the branches and sent a light shower of snow down on top of the truck. Piper laughed.

"It's like being in a snow globe!" she declared.

Cole followed a curve in the road, and then his house came into view. Joy inhaled softly, and Cole felt a renewed sense of pride in the sweet mountain home he'd helped to design and build.

"Is this where you live?" Piper asked, sitting up higher.

"This is it," he confirmed.

"It's lovely," Joy said. "Did you use one of Eldon's plans?"

"I started with one of his plans, and then we worked to-gether to modify it." He pulled the truck to a stop in front of the timber frame house. "I like the exposed joinery of post and beam, so I added more elaborate truss work than what Eldon typically designs."

He followed Joy's gaze to his house, trying to see it through her eyes. Built in rugged craftsman Montana style, it wasn't as sprawling as Eldon's house, but he'd managed to incorporate three bedrooms and three baths on the second floor, and a master suite on the first floor. The house was situated on the edge of the mountain, and commanded the same views across the valley to Flathead Lake that Eldon's house had.

"I like your red door," Piper declared.

"Thanks," he replied. "Why don't we go inside? I know six puppies who are very excited to meet you."

They went inside and, as they removed their coats and boots, Cole watched the expression on Joy's face as she looked around her. He saw wonder and delight, and then disbelief as she finally turned to look at him.

"Did you design this?"

"I did." He couldn't keep the pride out of his voice.

"It's amazing," she finally said. "I didn't expect it to be so big and bright."

She gazed around her at the open concept interior, with its cathedral ceilings, spanned by enormous timber beams. The kitchen opened directly to the living area, which was dominated by a massive stone fireplace, and there were views from every room through the soaring windows at the back of the house. His furnishings were simple, but comfortable. He'd used a warm, honey-hued Douglas fir for the walls and beams, while his kitchen cabinets were the same dark red as his front door.

"Can I see the puppies?" Piper asked, almost bouncing in her excitement.

"Follow me," Cole said, and led them through the living room to a closed door on the far side of the house, through which he could hear the muffled sounds of the puppies.

"This room was designed to be an office, but I've never been one for deskwork, so I use it mainly for storage." He grinned at Piper. "And for whelping pups. I keep the door closed while I'm gone, otherwise they'd just try to escape and then destroy the house."

Piper pressed against him, eager to see what lay beyond the closed door. With a flourish, he opened it for her and immediately there was the sound of excited squeals and barking. Piper gave an enthralled gasp and launched herself into the sea of squirming fur.

A yellow Labrador with a green collar heaved herself to her feet from where she'd been lying on an oversized dog bed, and came to greet them, her tail wagging.

"Hello, girl," Cole said, stroking her soft fur. "This is Lucy, the proud mama. And this rowdy bunch are her offspring."

Joy bent down to scoop one curious puppy into her arms. He wriggled uncontrollably and licked her everywhere he could reach. Joy laughed, and struggled to hold onto the writhing bundle. Cole watched how her face changed with her laughter, and it just about stole his breath away. Her gray-green eyes sparkled, and her smile was wide and genuine, revealing white teeth and shiny, pink gums.

"Oh, my goodness!" she gasped. Cole took pity on her and retrieved the puppy from her grasp. "I didn't expect them to be so big!"

Cole tucked the puppy into the crook of his arm and scratched him behind his ears. "Yeah, they're ready to go to their permanent homes. There's a young couple coming from Missoula in just a few days to get this guy. He's a Christmas gift for their little boy."

Piper looked up from where she sat on the floor, alternately embracing and fending off the canine onslaught, and her giggles of delight turned to dismay. "You're not keeping them?"

"Oh, honey, he can't possibly keep all of them," Joy said. "Seven dogs is a lot of responsibility."

"They'll be going to good homes," Cole assured the little girl, although there were still two pups that hadn't yet been claimed. "I expect they'll all be gone by Christmas, and then it will just be Lucy and me again."

Piper looked at Joy, and there was no mistaking the pleading in her blue eyes. Cole intercepted the warning look that Joy gave her daughter, and attempted to distract the little girl from what he knew would come next.

"Lucy probably needs to go out, and I need to feed these little guys," he said. He looked at Piper. "Want to help me put their food dishes together?"

"Yes!" Piper clambered to her feet, and Cole retrieved a baby gate from the hallway and barricaded the door. The puppies yipped and squealed as Cole led Joy and Piper into the kitchen, and Lucy padded along beside them.

Cole opened the door for Lucy, and then returned to the kitchen, where Piper perched on her knees on a stool at the island, waiting. Reaching into a lower cabinet, Cole retrieved two enormous stainless steel bowls and set them on the counter.

Piper's eyes widened. "Do they each get one of those?"

Cole laughed. "No, that would make them sick. I put enough puppy chow in each one for three puppies, and they share."

Joy came around the island to help him, and he liked her easy manner as she asked where she could find the puppy chow and the soft food he mixed into it. He measured out the dry food and watched as she deftly opened four cans of the food and slid them across the counter to him.

"Mr. Tanner," Piper said, gazing around at her surroundings. "How come you don't have a Christmas tree, neither?"

"Either," Joy corrected.

"How come?" she repeated. "Mommy said Montana is the best place to spend Christmas, because of the snow and the pine trees."

Cole pretended to be absorbed in mixing the puppy food. "Yup," he agreed. "Montana is a pretty special place during the holidays."

"But how come you don't have a Christmas tree?" she persisted. "Or any decorations?"

Cole glanced at Joy. She was rinsing out the empty cans under the faucet, but she spared him a swift, questioning glance. Cole hesitated. He didn't want to shatter the little girl's illusions about Christmas, but that was exactly what would happen if he told her that he didn't particularly enjoy celebrating the holiday. For him, it was a bittersweet reminder of the night when his father had slunk out of town, leaving Cole in a rundown motel room, sound asleep. While he'd never quite lost his aversion to Christmas, he'd at least actively participated in the festivities when he'd lived with Matt and his family. But with Matt gone, even that had stopped.

He typically volunteered to be on duty overnight at the fire station every Christmas Eve. Since he wasn't married and didn't have kids, it was no sacrifice for him to spend that time at the station. In fact, he preferred it. He and his firefighting buddies always cooked a hearty breakfast and a Christmas dinner for the guys and gals who were on duty.

Now he looked at Piper and shrugged. "I guess I haven't

had time to get a tree," he fibbed.

"Why?"

"Well, because I work a lot," he hedged, "and when I get home from work, all the Christmas tree shops are closed."

"Why?"

Cole cast a pleading look at Joy, but she merely leaned her elbows on the counter, watching him with interest.

"Well, I get home pretty late sometimes," he finally said.

"Why?"

Cole didn't know how much Piper knew about her father or how he had perished, so he was reluctant to tell the little girl that he was also a firefighter, in case it brought back any bad memories, for either her or her mother. He glanced at Joy, but she clearly wasn't going to help him with this.

"Listen," he said, knowing he was taking the coward's way out. "Let's do this. Your mom and I will carry the food bowls to the puppies, if you can go ahead of us and distract them. In fact, why don't you pick out a puppy to keep for yourself?" He didn't look at Joy. "But only if it's okay with your mom."

Piper let out an ear-piercing squeal of delight that, unless he'd heard it for himself, Cole never would have believed could come from such a tiny human. She was practically defibrillating with suppressed excitement as she turned to Joy.

"Can I, Mommy? Can I *pleease* keep one? I promise I'll take care of it. I'll feed it, and give it a bath, and take it for walks, and"—she wrinkled her nose—"even pick up the poop."

Joy gave Cole a look that clearly said she'd deal with him later, before schooling her expression and turning her attention to her daughter.

"I don't know, darling. How would we get it back to California?"

"He can go on the airplane with us, in a little cage," Piper said, her face alight with hope. "There was a lady on our plane who did that."

"But we have such a small apartment," Joy countered.

"He's just a small puppy!"

"Because he's still a baby. But he's going to grow until he—or she—is as big as Lucy."

Cole was beginning to realize the monumental error he'd just made, and what a difficult position he'd put Joy in.

"Does your apartment allow pets?" he asked.

"Yes!" Piper interjected. "Everyone in our building has a dog or a cat except us."

Seeing her daughter's indignant expression, Joy started to laugh. "Okay, okay." She threw her hands up in surrender. "Yes, let's do this. Go ahead. Go pick out a puppy and we'll bring it home with us. Why not?"

Piper gave a whoop of delight and flung her arms around Joy. "Thank you, thank you, thank you, Mommy! I promise I'll take care of him. You won't even know he's there!"

Cole watched as Piper ran out of the room, before turning his attention to Joy. "I'm sorry," he began, spreading his hands out. "I wasn't thinking, and I put you in a tough spot."

Joy waved away his protests. "No, it actually works out

for the best. Piper only asked for three things for Christmas, and a puppy was number two on her list. The first was a white Christmas, and I think that's been covered."

"What was the third thing she asked for?"

Joy gave him a wide smile, but there was an unmistakable sheen of moisture in her eyes.

"A new daddy."

Chapter Five

JOY MIGHT HAVE laughed at the expression on Cole's face, if she didn't think he actually believed she might be considering him as a possible candidate to fulfill the third request on Piper's Christmas list.

"Don't look so worried," she said, unable to suppress her smile. "I'm not in the market for a husband, so you're completely safe."

Cole picked up the two bowls of puppy chow. "I don't know whether to be relieved or insulted."

Without waiting for Joy to respond, he carried the bowls into the next room. Joy leaned against the counter and absently wiped her moist eyes, wondering what had just happened. Had she just been outmaneuvered into keeping one of the puppies, or had it really been her own decision? And in the end, did it really matter?

Her daughter was happy, and another Christmas wish had been fulfilled. Pushing away from the counter, she started to follow Cole, when a movement by the kitchen window caught her attention. Curious, she leaned over the sink and peered out.

A hummingbird hovered just outside, although there

were no bird feeders in sight. Joy felt her mouth fall open. She turned and called Cole's name. But when she turned back, the tiny bird was gone, and Joy wondered if she had imagined it.

A scratching at the door alerted her that Lucy was ready to come back indoors, and Joy opened the door to let the dog inside. Then, with a last, wondering look at where she had seen the hummingbird, she closed the door and crossed the house to where Cole and Piper were watching the puppies eat. Piper sat on the floor while two of the puppies crawled all over her, whining in their eagerness to lick her face.

Cole leaned against the doorframe, a smile on his face. He turned as Joy approached.

"Did you call me?"

Joy shook her head. "It was nothing."

"Listen," he said, lowering his voice, "if you don't want to do this, then let me know now. I'm sure we can figure something out. Adopting a puppy isn't for everyone."

"Thanks," Joy said drily, "but I think we're a little past that. Look at her."

"She does look pretty happy," Cole agreed. "So, what made you give in so easily?"

Joy looked at him, wondering just how much she should share with him. What she felt was intensely personal. She'd only spoken about Matt's death and how it had impacted her, to her mother and her closest friends. She drew in a deep breath.

"Please don't misunderstand me, but after Matt died, I

made a decision not to take life so seriously." She risked a glance at Cole. He still watched Piper and the puppies, but a small frown knitted his brow. "Let me explain. I lived with sorrow for a long time after he passed. Piper was barely two years old, so she didn't understand what had happened. I tried to act normal for her but the truth is, the grief nearly crushed me. Grief doesn't say, *I've been here for long enough; it's time for me to leave.*' Grief lays right on your heart as you wake up, and demands to be felt. I slept with it, walked with it, cried with it while driving in my car. It planted a seed in me, and it grew. I could have let it live inside me, growing bigger, forever. I could have let it consume me."

"But?" he prompted.

"But I had a sweet little daughter to raise, and I needed normalcy—real normalcy, not the forced kind—in my life for her sake." She stopped to draw in a deep breath. Even after all these years, she found it hard to remember those days when sadness and the hollowness of aching loss had been her constant companions. "I think grief is a price you will inevitably pay when you love, but you can also learn from it."

"What did you learn?" His voice had a rough edge to it.

"I learned to let it go. Even though I know it will visit me again in my lifetime, I came to the realization that it was time for sorrow to leave. I had to start imagining a life where I was *alive*." She turned to look at him. "So I made a conscious decision not to take life so seriously, and if that means adopting a puppy at a time that might not be perfectly convenient for me, then so be it."

"I admire your ability to move on," he said. "I really do."

Joy frowned. "You make it sound as if I've forgotten Matt. I'll never forget him, and I don't want to. He gave me the very best of himself." She looked meaningfully at Piper, who had her father's bright hair, his blue eyes, and his easy ability to laugh deeply and often. "He wouldn't want me to bury myself in grief. He would want me to be happy. Maybe it took losing him to finally know how I want to live."

"Impulsively?" he asked wryly.

"Joyfully."

"Mommy, I want this one!"

Their conversation was interrupted as Piper scrambled to her feet, clutching a puppy that was almost too heavy for her to lift.

"Let me take a look," Cole said.

Joy watched as he stepped away from her and bent to examine the puppy. "This one is perfect for you," he finally declared. "He's a boy, and he was actually the last one that was born in this litter, so I've always called him Number Six."

Piper laughed. "That's a funny name."

The puppy licked her chin, as if in agreement.

"You can give him a new name," Cole suggested.

Piper considered for a moment. "Snowflake?"

Cole raised an eyebrow. "Does he look like a snowflake to you?"

"No. How about Fluffy?" The puppy barked and then shook its head, making his little ears flap. Piper laughed. "I don't think he likes that name, either!"

"We don't have to give him a name right now," Joy assured her. "We can think about it for a day or two."

But Piper's face had already lit up with a new idea. "I know! I'll name him Montana! Then I'll always remember where he came from."

"Montana," Cole mused thoughtfully. "That has a nice ring to it."

"I love it," Joy declared. "It's a perfect name for a perfect dog."

"Montana!" Piper cried, and squeezed her arms around the puppy, which gave a small yip of happiness and proceeded to slather the little girl's face with wet kisses.

"I'll bring him around later today," Cole said. "I'll pick up some supplies for him first, and make sure you have everything you need for the little guy."

"Oh, you don't have to do that," Joy protested. "We can get whatever he needs."

"It's no trouble. I have to head into town later, anyway."

"Can we come, too?" Piper asked. "I can help you pick out a collar for Montana!"

Cole shrugged. "Sure, why not? We can check out the festival while we're there." He looked at Joy for her approval. "Does that sound like something you'd like to do?"

Joy looked at Piper and laughed. "I don't think it's up to me, but yes—it sounds perfect."

"Yay!" Piper let the puppy down, and then sat down on the floor to embrace as many of them as she could, giggling helplessly as they clambered over her.

"They're going to have a great friendship," Cole commented, watching as Montana barked happily at Piper.

"Well, at least let me pay you for him," Joy persisted. "These puppies look like purebreds, and I'm sure you could get a good price for him if you sold him."

"It's not about the money," he replied. "I enjoy sending good dogs to good homes. Besides"—he lowered his voice—"a puppy was on Piper's Christmas list, so consider it a gift from one of Santa's helpers."

"You? Santa's helper?" Joy looked at him, and couldn't quite suppress a grin. With his height, broad shoulders, and ruggedly handsome face, he was a far cry from any of the Santa's helpers she had seen during the busy holiday season.

Seeing her expression, Cole gave a rueful laugh. "Okay, so maybe I'm a little tall to be an elf, but I really want her to have the puppy. Something tells me they were meant to be together."

The smile transformed his face and made him seem younger. Joy hadn't seen him smile very often, and thought he'd experienced his share of sorrow, too. She knew the Hollidays had taken him into their home because his father had abandoned him when he'd been a little boy. That kind of betrayal had to make an impact on how he viewed life. Maybe she wasn't the only one who needed to learn how to live joyfully.

AFTER A STOP at the local pet store, where Piper selected a bright red collar for the puppy, and Cole purchased the other essentials they would need to care for him, they drove into town. The downtown region of Glacier Creek had been closed to vehicle traffic and turned into a pedestrian only Christmas festival. Cole found a place to park on a side street, behind The Ginger Snap, a bakery owned by Dana Marshall, the fiancée of one of his firefighting buddies. He guessed she would have a booth in the festival, but just in case Piper didn't get her fill of sweets as they strolled through the Christmas market, they could always stop at the bakery for a cup of hot chocolate and a cookie before heading home.

Cole lifted Piper down from the cab, and Joy took her hand as they made their way through the narrow alley between the bakery and The Curiosity Shop, a vintage boutique that was popular with Beth and the other ladies in town. As they emerged from the alley, the entire length of Main Street was lined with vendor tents and booths selling arts and crafts, beeswax candles, wooden ornaments, mulled cider, bratwurst, homemade soap, and other goodies. At the far end of Main Street, the road ended in a small parking area, where a long, wide pier extended out over the lake and bright ice-fishing huts dotted the frozen surface.

The center common, which divided Main Street into two one-way streets, had been strung with Christmas lights and contained both a skating rink and a Santa's Village, complete with a towering Christmas tree decorated in gold and silver. Festive bunting of sparkling white lights and oversized snowflakes had been hung over the streets, and the storefronts were decked with cedar boughs and silver bells.

A group of carolers, dressed in Victorian clothing, stood

in the center of the common, near the gazebo, singing Christmas songs. The tantalizing aroma of kettle corn, hotdogs, and warm pretzels permeated the frosty air, and throngs of people made their way slowly through the festival, sipping hot cider or hot chocolate.

"The town plows must have worked through the night to clear the snow," Joy marveled. "How did they manage to get everything set up in time?"

"That's actually where I was headed last night when we almost collided," Cole said. "We're accustomed to snowstorms, but the town really pulled together to make the festival happen."

"They do this every year?"

"They haven't missed a year since I've been here, and that was more than twenty years ago."

They spent the next hour walking the length of the festival along one side of the common, sampling the food and admiring the many different items for sale. Cole didn't normally browse the festival—he generally avoided anything that revolved around the celebration of Christmas—but found himself enjoying Joy's company, however reluctantly. He'd been so prepared to keep her at arm's length, but that was difficult to do when she took such obvious delight in everything at the festival. She even seemed to like his company. Piper delighted over the handmade toys, as well as the food items, and Cole admired how Joy handled the child's numerous requests, allowing her to have a warm pretzel, but not a sugary funnel cake, and telling her that they wouldn't buy any of the toys, because it was too close to Christmas.

Cole knew almost everyone at the festival, and saw by their curious glances and cheerful greetings they wondered who the pretty woman and little girl were by his side. He was reluctant to introduce Joy. He didn't want anyone to think they were a couple. They stopped at the Ginger Snap bakery tent when Joy insisted on buying a half dozen apple turnovers for the following morning, and he had no choice but to introduce her to Dana Marshall.

"Welcome to Glacier Creek," Dana said, smiling at Joy. "I'm a transplant, too, from Arizona."

"Oh, well, my daughter and I don't plan to live here," Joy said, looking embarrassed. "We're only here for the holiday, and then we're returning to California."

"Okay, sure," Dana replied, and winked at Piper. "That's what I said, too, but then I met a hunky firefighter named Scott Ross, and the rest is history." She held out her hand to show Joy a large diamond solitaire on one finger. "We're getting married in the spring."

"Congratulations," Joy replied, but Cole thought her enthusiasm sounded strained.

"How about a ginger snap for you?" Dana asked, looking at Piper. "They're my specialty."

"Yes, please," Piper said politely, and gave Dana a toothless grin when she was given one for each hand.

"How come you're not manning the Christmas tree lot with the rest of the crew?" Dana asked, looking at Cole.

While Cole didn't typically patronize the festival, he usually volunteered to sell Christmas trees and wreaths at the lot operated by the Glacier Creek forest service station. All the proceeds went to a good cause, and Cole enjoyed hanging out with the other firefighters who volunteered.

"I'll be there tomorrow," he said, "but thought I'd spend today showing Joy and Piper around."

"Maybe the four of us can get together for a holiday drink at The Drop Zone," Dana said. "I'll mention it to Scott."

Cole made a noncommittal reply, aware of Joy's discomfort. They said their goodbyes, but stopped several more times to exchange pleasantries with other vendors and townspeople that Cole knew. By the time they reached the end of the first street, Piper began to visibly flag.

"Maybe we should head back," Joy suggested. "I think someone is getting tired, and it's very cold outside."

"No, I'm not tired," Piper protested, but when Cole picked her up, she put her arms around his neck and laid her head on his shoulder with an enormous yawn.

"I can carry her," Joy offered, but Cole shook his head.

"Nope, I've got her."

The little girl was a warm, sleepy weight in his arms as they made their way back to the truck.

"That was fun," Joy said. "Thank you for bringing us."

"It was my pleasure," Cole replied, and realized it was the truth.

When Beth had first told him that Joy would be coming to Glacier Creek for Christmas, he'd been prepared to dislike her. He'd already had six years to resent her, first for enticing Matt into leaving Montana, and then for keeping Piper in California after Matt died, denying Beth and Eldon the opportunity to spend more time with their only grandchild.

But the more time he spent in her company, the more he liked her. Beth had told him Joy was only twenty-seven years old, but she seemed more mature than most women her age. Cole guessed that came from losing her husband and becoming a single mom overnight, when most of her friends were probably still hitting the bars and hooking up with guys they barely knew. She was a good mother. He couldn't fault her for refusing to uproot her daughter and move to Montana, far away from everything that was familiar to her. However reluctantly, Cole found himself revising his earlier opinion of Joy.

It also didn't hurt that she was so damned pretty. He'd had his share of relationships, most of which hadn't worked out because of his job, which took him away for long periods of time during the summer months. But, in retrospect, most of the women he'd dated hadn't been interested in a long-term commitment. Maybe that was why he'd been attracted to them in the first place, because he hadn't been remotely interested in settling down.

But there was something about Joy that made him want that kind of relationship. She acted reserved around him, and he sensed she wasn't completely comfortable in his company. He wanted to change that. He wanted to see her let her guard down. He wanted to see her smile. He wanted to hear her laugh, the way she'd laughed at his house earlier that day, with the puppies. More than that, he wanted to be the one to make her smile.

They had reached the truck, and Joy opened the door on

the passenger side.

"She's sound asleep," Joy said.

"Will this wake her up?"

"I doubt it. This has been a pretty exciting day for her, so I think she's pretty zonked."

Cole carefully shifted her into his arms, and lifted Piper into her car seat. Her cheeks were bright pink, and she mumbled incoherently when he buckled her in, but she didn't wake up. She looked small and vulnerable, and a wave of protectiveness swept over him. In his line of work, he was accustomed to protecting people, but he'd never had the urge to take care of another person. He drove carefully back to the Holliday house, trying to avoid the potholes and uneven terrain, not wanting to wake the little girl up.

"You don't have to worry," Joy said in an amused tone. "Trust me, she is not going to wake up. Once she's down, she's down for the count. She'll sleep for at least a couple of hours."

Cole relaxed marginally. "Is she in kindergarten yet?"

"She just started in September. She only goes in the morning, but it's been such a boon for me. I can finally get some work done."

"What is it you do?" He knew almost nothing about Joy, except that she was Matt's widow and Piper's mother.

"I'm an artist."

"Oh? What kind of artist?" Cole had once been tricked into attending a viewing at a local art gallery, and he still had an occasional nightmare about the event.

Call him Neanderthal, but he had an immediate image

of big canvasses streaked with globules of paint that had been flung rather than placed with any kind of deliberation. How anyone could call that art was beyond him. Five-year-old Piper could probably do better.

"I'm a ceramic artist."

"As in hand-thrown pottery?"

"Yes. I have several designs, and they're actually quite popular in Santa Barbara, and along the Pacific coast. There are a dozen or so shops that carry my work."

Cole recalled seeing the glaze ware in Beth's kitchen, in deep shades of foggy gray, blue, and forest green. Beth had an entire set of the dishware, and used it for everything, but Cole had never thought to ask where she had gotten it. Something told him that Joy had made the pottery.

He pulled his eyes from the road to give her a quick look of admiration. "Beth has a set."

"She does. I was just getting my business up and running when I met Matt, and the pattern that Beth has is one of my first."

"She loves that dishware."

Joy laughed. "I know. Every time she comes to visit, she buys another place setting, or more mugs, or a serving bowl. I try to gift everything to her, but she always insists on paying me for it. I actually created some complementary patterns to give her more choices."

"Were those your dishes that we used at breakfast this morning?"

"They were, actually."

Cole looked at her, surprised. "And you never said a

word!"

Joy laughed. "Well, what would I say? *Gee, I really love this pottery?* I'm just happy she likes it and uses it."

"She has some dishes with flowers on them. Did you do those, too?"

"I'll have to see which ones you mean, but if they have irises on them, or lupines, then yes. The colors go well with the glaze on her original set, and add a little something special, I think."

"That's pretty impressive," Cole said. "How many different designs do you make?"

"Just five."

"How do you find the time to do all that, while raising a child?"

"I have a potter's studio, and because the demand has increased over the past few years, I recently started a program where I teach pottery to local students. If they're interested, they can apply to become an intern in my studio, creating pieces for my different lines."

"How has that worked out?"

"Overall, pretty good. I have a few students who create really beautiful work for me, and then others who are still learning. Their work is good, but might have small flaws. I sell those pieces at a discounted price, and they get a portion of the proceeds. Once they become masters, they receive a larger percentage of the proceeds." Joy shrugged. "I prefer to throw my own pieces, but the students really help to keep my inventory up. I earn enough to make ends meet, so I can't complain."

They turned onto the mountain road, and Cole realized they would soon be home. He didn't want the day to end. He'd already monopolized both Joy and Piper for the entire day, and guilt gnawed at him, knowing Beth and Eldon hadn't had much opportunity to spend time with their granddaughter. An idea was formulating in his head, and he told himself it had nothing to do with Joy, and everything to do with letting Eldon and Beth spend some quality time with Piper.

He told himself he was taking one for the team.

"I know you only just arrived in Glacier Creek," he began cautiously, "but I thought you might like to get out tonight and experience some of the local color. They have live music at The Drop Zone, and the food's pretty good, too."

"Oh, I don't know," she said doubtfully. "I have Piper to think about. She might be nervous if I leave her."

Cole persisted. "I'll bring her puppy over after she's had her supper. Something tells me she won't even notice you're gone. Besides, it might be nice for Beth and Eldon to have her to themselves for a bit. I know Beth has been dying for a chance to spoil her, just a little."

He glanced over at her, and could see she was considering his words. She looked at her sleeping daughter, and then at Cole, and she nodded.

"Okay, that sounds nice."

She'd agreed.

He wouldn't let himself think about why his spirits suddenly felt lighter than they had in months. This was just a way to give Beth some time with Piper. He still had unanswered questions, and he wasn't convinced Joy was as perfect as she appeared to be.

"Great." He allowed himself a measured smile. "I'll drop you both off, and then come back around six thirty."

They pulled up in front of the house, and Cole was out of the truck and around to the passenger side before Joy had a chance to open her door. He helped her down, and then reached in for Piper. The little girl barely stirred as he lifted her out of the car seat. Joy went ahead of him to open the door of the house, and Beth came out to greet them.

"Oh, the sweet little thing," she said, upon seeing Piper's limp form. "Let's bring her in by the fire. She can sleep right on the sofa next to me."

Cole laid Piper down against the sofa pillows, and Beth bent over her, gently removing her boots, coat and hat. Joy walked with him back to the door.

"Thank you again for everything," she said. "For the puppy, and for a lovely day at the festival."

"You're welcome. I'll see you tonight."

As she closed the door behind him, Cole strode to his truck, his thoughts already on the coming evening. He had to remind himself it wasn't a date. They'd only just met.

A cracking sound behind him caught his attention, and he turned just in time to see an enormous icicle break loose from the overhang on the house and crash onto the ground below. Cole eyed it with suspicion. But as he reversed the truck and drove away, he knew he was in big trouble, because the icicle wasn't the only thing beginning to thaw.

Chapter Six

THE DROP ZONE pub was just starting to get busy when they arrived at seven o'clock. The entire roof and building had been outlined with bright Christmas lights. An enormous Christmas tree, strung with white lights and decorated with red Christmas balls and firefighting ornaments, dominated the wide entry.

Cole pushed through the doors, the noise and music and smells as familiar to him as an old friend. He indicated a high-top table near the bar.

"Let's sit over there. We can still see the band and the dance floor, but our eardrums won't suffer!"

Joy nodded, and made her way through the pub to the table he had indicated. He took her coat and draped it alongside his on one of the empty chairs, placing his hat on top. The Drop Zone was a popular drinking spot for the locals, and Cait, the owner's daughter, did a pretty good job in the kitchen.

There were a number of couples eating dinner, and nearly every bar stool was occupied. Cole recognized several guys from the fire station, including Tyler Dodson, one of the more seasoned smokejumpers. He raised a hand in a brief acknowledgment when they nodded at him. They'd subject him to the third-degree once he returned to the base station, but for now they gave him and Joy some privacy.

"This place has a fun vibe!" Joy seated herself at the table and looked around with interest. "I can see why it's a favorite."

Cole took the seat adjacent to Joy. He indicated the fifty-foot oak bar that ran the entire length of one wall.

"That bar was rescued from a former brothel in the old mining town of Taft."

Joy laughed. "Wow, that's very cool. I like the tin ceilings."

Cole glanced upward, trying to see the pub through her eyes.

He'd been coming to The Drop Zone for so long, he no longer noticed the details that made the place so unique. The tin ceilings overhead were gold, and embossed with scenes from the gold rush. The walls were hung with an assortment of firefighting posters, including one that read, *It's not a party until the fire department shows up.* A vintage juke box cranked out country music and, from the room at the back of the pub, Cole could hear the ricochet of balls as groups of people shot pool at the two tables.

"Yeah, the place certainly has character," he agreed.

The pub had a coziness to it that made people want to stay, and tonight they had a fire going in the rustic fireplace. A wreath had been hung over the mantle, and a long string of mini-lights in the shape of firefighting helmets had been strung over the bar. On the far side of the dance floor, a small band was making the final adjustments to their equipment.

Joy reached for the drink menu and made a show of studying it. "Did you come here often with Matt?"

Cole hunched his shoulders against the unbidden memories. He and Matt had spent more time in this pub than he cared to admit.

"All the firefighters came here," he said, his voice rough. "Matt was no different."

But he had been different, because he'd been one of the few smokejumpers who had been raised in Glacier Creek, but had chosen to leave. Not only had he left Montana, but he'd given up jumping and had worked the wildfires from the ground, instead.

Matt had wanted to be a wildland firefighter for as far back as Cole could recall, and because he'd made it sound so appealing, Cole had followed him into the line of work. He counted himself lucky he'd been accepted into the training program at the Glacier Creek base. He'd been able to establish a career for himself in the small town he'd adopted as his own. Both he and Matt had been accepted into the smokejumper training program, and Matt had been a favorite with the brass. Cole thought he might have even made captain one day, had he not relocated to California.

"So, what do you do in the winter, when there are no fires to battle?" Joy asked. "Plow the roads?"

"Nah," Cole said. "That's just a ruse I use to meet pretty women, by running them off the road."

Pink color bloomed in her cheeks.

"I'm kidding," he said, more seriously. "I'm a seasonal firefighter, so I work my butt off for six months, jumping fires all over the country, and then I have six months off."

"So what do you do during those six months?"

"When I'm not helping Eldon with the timber frame business, I do some ice-fishing on the lake, and I ski as much powder as I possibly can. I take small groups off-piste for a more extreme ski experience."

"That means off-trail, right?"

"Have you ever skied?"

"Never," Joy said, looking slightly alarmed. "Until I came to Montana, I'd never been more than a hundred miles from the Pacific Ocean."

"If you're interested," he suggested, "maybe I can take you—and Piper—up to the mountain. I'd be happy to give you both a day of lessons."

"I'm sure Piper would love that," she said, smiling.

"But not you?"

She cringed. "I don't know... maybe? I'm not very adventurous."

Privately, Cole disagreed. "What do you call starting your own business at the age of, what, twenty-one?"

"That's different."

"Why? Because you were doing something you enjoyed? I call it adventurous. Besides, didn't you tell me earlier today that you're trying not to take life so seriously?"

Joy laughed. "Wow. That seems like ages ago." She wrinkled her nose. "Was that really just today?"

"Yes, ma'am. Time does fly when you're having a good

time."

As he'd hoped, Joy laughed, and he couldn't help but grin back.

"How long do you think you'll jump wildfires?" she asked.

The question was casual, but he recognized the underlying anxiety in her voice. She probably worried that if something happened to him, there would be no one to keep an eye on Beth and Eldon as they grew older.

"There are guys on the crew who've been jumping fires for twenty years. As long as you keep yourself in shape, and can pass the fitness test, you can keep jumping. But I've given some thought to becoming a full-time partner at Holliday Homes," he said. "I enjoy the work, and—"

The waitress came then, interrupting the direction of the conversation. Not that it mattered. Why would she be interested in his hopes and dreams? He hadn't told anyone Eldon had asked him to take over the timber frame business, and it was probably better if he kept that information to himself until he'd made a decision.

They each ordered a beer and a burger. The band began to play a popular country song, and several couples got up to dance. Cole noticed Joy's shoulders moving in time to the music.

"Would you like to dance?" he asked.

Without giving her time to reply, he stood up and pulled her chair out. She looked surprised, but took his hand as he led her onto the small dance floor. The other couples were moving around the floor in a series of coordinated steps and turns.

"Wait," she said, tugging him to a stop. "I don't know how to country dance."

"I'll show you," Cole said, and pulled her into his arms. "We'll start with the two-step. It's the easiest thing in the world."

Seeing her doubtful expression, he placed her left hand on his upper arm, and took her right hand in his, keeping a small distance between their bodies. He dipped his head to look at her.

"Follow my lead," he said. "Quick, quick, slow, slow."

He demonstrated several steps, until she looked up at him in wonder.

"Am I doing it?" she asked, a smile spreading across her face.

"You are," he confirmed, moving her across the floor in time to the music. "You are killing the two-step."

Joy laughed, stumbled, but Cole immediately compensated and they were back in step.

"You make it seem so easy," she said, smiling up at him.

"You're a natural," he assured her. "If you'd like, I can show you how to do a spin, or a dip."

"Maybe next time," she said. "I'm very happy doing this for now."

Cole had to agree he was pretty happy doing this, too. He couldn't stop looking at her. Her gray-green eyes sparkled, and there was a light flush of color across her cheekbones. She wore her hair down tonight, and it fell around her shoulders in silky, brown waves. Cole wondered what it would feel like sliding through his fingers, and had to curl his hand around hers to keep from finding out. The song was coming to an end, so Cole released her with one hand, spinning her away from him before pulling her back into his arms, with her back against his chest.

Joy laughed, breathless. "I wasn't expecting that!"

"That move was called the sweetheart," Cole said, releasing her. "We'll have you doing country round dances in no time."

They returned to their table to find two frosty mugs of beer waiting for them, and Cole watched as Joy took a long swallow.

"Mmm," she said appreciatively. "That tastes good."

Cole looked up to see Dana Marshall from the Ginger Snap Bakery approaching their table with her fiancé. Cole stood up and gave Dana a hug, and then shook hands with her companion.

"Joy, I'd like you to meet to Scott Ross, and you met Dana in town earlier."

"This is your fiancé?" Joy asked, and shook Scott's hand.

"That's me," he confirmed with a grin. "We actually met right here at The Drop Zone. She was here on vacation with some girlfriends, and we spent a couple of days together. When it came time for her to leave, I persuaded her to stay."

"I was telling Scott that you're in town for the holidays," Dana said. "If you bring your little girl into the shop, the hot chocolate and dessert are on me. Oh, I almost forgot! We're doing a fundraiser for the festival, decorating gingerbread houses over at the Snapdragon Inn." She smiled. "I think your little girl would love it, and I made all the gingerbread myself."

"How did you end up owning the bakery?" Joy asked.

"My degree is in culinary arts, and after I made the decision to stay, I got a job working at the bakery," Dana replied. "About nine months later the owner, Dot, suffered a heart attack and decided to sell the business." She looked at Scott. "Sometimes it's about being in the right place at the right time."

Scott gave her a one-armed hug. "Well, we just wanted to come over and say hello. Welcome to Glacier Creek, Joy, and hope you have a good Christmas."

Their burgers arrived, and they ate in silence for a few moments, sharing a basket of fries.

"This has been a really nice day," Joy said, taking another sip of her beer. "I can't remember the last time I did something like this."

"Don't you date?"

Cole wasn't sure he wanted to hear the answer, but he couldn't believe the guys in California weren't knocking down her door for the chance to take her out. She was pretty, and smart, and a good mom. A guy would have to be a complete moron not to see how perfect she was.

Joy shrugged. "I've been on a couple of dates, but none of them resulted in a second date. I've learned that most guys aren't interested in a woman with a small child, and once they find out about Piper, they run for the hills."

"Then you're obviously meeting the wrong kind of men," Cole said. "Out here, we're a little smarter—we happen to like package deals."

Joy laughed, and she looked embarrassed by his words. Then her eyes turned curious, as if she couldn't quite figure him out. "I think today was a really nice day for Piper, too," she finally said. "You made her so happy by giving her that puppy."

"Piper's a great kid," he said. "She deserves to be happy."

They both deserved to be happy.

"Can I ask you a personal question?" she asked.

"Shoot."

"What happened to your parents?"

That was the last question he'd expected Joy to ask, and it took Cole by surprise. For a moment, he wasn't sure how to answer.

"Matt never told you?"

"Not everything," she replied. "He told me that your father worked at the sawmill and that he abandoned you, and they took you in. He said he didn't know all the details, and it wasn't something the family really talked much about. He said you never talked about it, and he never wanted to ask."

Twenty-one years had passed since Cole's father had left him, and although Cole told himself he'd gotten over it, he realized the memory still had the power to hurt him and make him feel like that small, lost boy again. What kind of man abandoned his only child, and on Christmas Eve no less?

"I'm sorry," Joy said. "I don't mean to pry, and it's none of my business."

"No," Cole said. "It's okay." He squared his shoulders,

mentally preparing himself to dredge up the unpleasant memories. "My mother died when I was a baby. I don't remember anything about her. My father said she had cancer, and that she went quickly."

"I'm so sorry." Joy's face reflected her sympathy. "Did you live here, in Glacier Creek?"

"No, I think my parents were from Florida, but I'm not actually sure." Seeing her puzzled expression, he tried to explain. "We moved around a lot. My father chased different jobs, never sticking with one for longer than a year. We'd stay in one spot just long enough for me to finish a school year, and then we'd be on the road again."

"That must have been incredibly difficult," Joy said. "I can't imagine doing that to a child!"

Cole shrugged. "I don't think I minded. It was all I knew, and as long as I had my dad, I was okay. Then we came to Glacier Creek, and he got a job working at the sawmill."

"Eldon's sawmill," Joy clarified.

"That's right. I went to the local elementary school, and because we were living in a motel on the outskirts of town, I took the school bus to Matt's house each day and then rode home with my dad."

"That's how you became friends with Matt?"

"Yep. He was a year older than me, so we weren't in the same class at school, but we became inseparable. We started hanging out his house after school instead of the lumberyard, and Beth would feed me." He grinned. "I was always hungry."

"So what happened? Why did your dad leave?"

Cole shrugged. "He had his demons. I don't know what they were, but he couldn't stay put for very long. Something was going on with him, but I don't know what it was. I saw the signs, and knew he was getting ready to hit the road again. This time, he wasn't even waiting for the end of the school year." He grew silent for a moment, remembering. "The day before Christmas, we had a huge fight. I told him that I hated him, and that I wanted to stay in Glacier Creek."

"Oh, Cole." Her voice was soft.

"I went to bed so angry at him, and woke up on Christmas morning to find him gone. No note, no explanation. Just eighty-three dollars on top of the dresser. I sat alone in that motel room for hours, thinking any minute he'd come back. But he never did."

There was a moment of utter silence as she stared at him in dismay. He understood; she couldn't comprehend how a parent could abandon a child. She was raising Piper the way she'd been raised—with unselfish love. She would do anything for her child.

"What did you do?"

Cole had never talked about his father with anyone outside of the Holliday family, although most of the people in Glacier Creek were aware of what had happened. He preferred not to think about that time, but something about Joy made him want to share the story with her. Her manner said she empathized with him, without pitying him.

"We'd been invited to have Christmas dinner with Eldon

and Beth, and when we didn't show up, Eldon and Matt drove to the motel to find out why. They took me back to their house, and I stayed." He gave her what he hoped was a careless grin. "And I've been here ever since."

Joy was staring at him as if she'd never seen him before. "Wow," she finally said. "What happened to your father? Was he okay?"

That part of the story was the most painful for Cole, and over the years, people had expressed their sympathy, shock, and even anger over his father's actions. What they'd said about Harley Ray Tanner hadn't been complimentary. Cole had learned to respond with an offhand shrug and even a joke, as if he couldn't care less his father had abandoned him the way someone would an unwanted pup.

With Joy, however, he had difficulty maintaining an indifferent attitude. His father's actions that Christmas Eve had been the most hurtful that Cole had ever experienced. Harley had been a hard man, but for all his faults, he'd been a good father and Cole had loved him. He'd silently cried himself to sleep for weeks afterwards, convinced he had been the cause of his father's rejection.

"I don't know what happened to him. He never came back," he said simply. "Eldon hired a private investigator to find him, without any luck. He was a seasonal worker who got paid cash under the table for his work at the sawmill, so there weren't any records of him at the office. I know Eldon did everything he could to find him, but after a couple of years, we stopped looking."

"So you have no idea what happened to him after he left

Glacier Creek?" Joy sat back in her chair, disbelief written on her face.

"I've done some internet searches over the years," Cole admitted, "but I've never come up with anything solid. It's like he just dropped off the face of the earth."

"What about extended family?"

"I'm embarrassed to admit that I don't even know my mother's maiden name. Dad only ever called her *Elaine*." He shrugged. "I was just a kid, and it wasn't anything we ever talked about. She died, he was stuck with me, end of story."

Joy reached across the table and grabbed his hand, her eyes full of sympathy. "I'm so sorry that happened to you," she said. "You didn't deserve it. But I honestly believe that everything happens for a reason, even if that reason isn't always apparent to us."

Privately, Cole thought that was a bunch of horse manure, but he wasn't going to offend Joy, so he simply nodded.

"Yeah. Sure."

She withdrew her hand and sat back to consider him. "You don't believe me."

Cole leaned over the table and lowered his voice. "I wasn't going to say anything, but here it is. There are some things I can't make rhyme nor reason of, no matter how hard I try, and there's no way anyone is ever going to convince me those things happened for a reason, or that something good is ever going to come from them. I'm not buying it. Bad stuff happens, end of story."

"I understand," she said, "but I think something good

already has come of it. You see, if your father had taken you back on the road when you were eight, you might not have returned to Glacier Creek. You wouldn't have purchased land from Eldon, or built that beautiful house. Piper wouldn't have her puppy." She paused, and warm color tinged her neck and cheeks. "And I might never have met you."

As much as he'd have liked to disagree, Cole couldn't argue with her. Everything she'd said was true. As they finished their meal, and their conversation turned to more everyday subjects, like the Glacier Creek Christmas Festival, and Joy's work as a potter, Cole's mind kept going back to what she'd said.

I might never have met you.

He didn't quite know what to make of that. Was she glad she'd met him? Was she attracted to him? He hoped like hell that was the case, because he could no longer deny he liked being with her. More than liked it, if he was being honest. He liked watching the expressions on her face, and liked hearing her laugh.

As the evening drew to a close, and he pulled up in front of the Holliday house, it was just past ten o'clock. The lamp post at the end of the walk had been left on, and there were lights on in the house, although Cole guessed that everyone inside had long since gone to bed.

"I'll walk you to the door," he said, as Joy opened the passenger side door and climbed out.

He left the truck engine running, and the frozen snow crunched under their boots as they walked to the house. At the door, Joy turned and looked at him, her face partially shadowed.

"I had a really nice time tonight, Cole," she said.

"Yeah, I had a good time, too," he said, and jammed his hands into the pockets of his shearling coat to keep from reaching for her. "Will I see you—and Piper—tomorrow?"

"I'd like that," she said. "I told Piper we'd begin decorating the house, and baking cookies." She gave him a shy smile. "You're more than welcome to help."

"Ah, I almost forgot that I'm volunteering at the festival tomorrow, selling trees for the base station. Maybe I'll stop by after."

"Or maybe we'll come into town and see the rest of the festival," she replied, her smile widening.

"I'd like that," he said. "I'll keep an eye out for you."

They stood looking at each other for a long minute, before Joy mumbled a good-night and turned to go inside.

"Joy," he said, and caught her arm.

She turned back to him, her face expectant.

Before he lost his nerve, he bent his head and brushed his lips across hers in the briefest of contact.

"Goodnight," he said brusquely, and strode back to his truck before he was tempted to kiss her more thoroughly.

He waited until she was safely indoors and had snapped the outside light off before he thrust the truck into gear, and turned in the direction of his own house.

The kiss had been nothing, he told himself. But something told him he'd lie awake that night for a long time, thinking about nothing.

Chapter Seven

J OY AND PIPER spent the following morning in the kitchen with Grammy, baking cookies. Piper wore one of her grandmother's aprons over a tulle skirt of sparkly silver, and spent more time sampling the finished products than actually helping to create them. She moved from one end of the island to the other, depending on where the best tasting opportunities were, while Montana tried to pounce on the trailing end of her apron strings, barking with excitement. Even Eldon joined in, helping Piper spread frosting on the cookies, and then showing her how to decorate them with the dozens of festive toppings that Beth had provided.

After the first several batches had been decorated and packed into airtight containers, Piper lost interest in both baking and eating the cookies. Instead, she sat on a stool at the island, watching as Beth cooked fudge on the stovetop, and Joy measured out the ingredients for gingerbread cookies.

"Mommy, can I go outside and play with Montana?" she asked, teasing the puppy with a nylon pull-rope that Cole had included in the basket of supplies he had brought over. "I think he has to go."

"Can you wait just two more minutes?" Joy asked. "I have cookies that are almost ready to come out of the oven."

Getting Piper bundled into her outdoor gear could take up to fifteen minutes, depending on how wriggly or helpful she decided to be.

Eldon stood up from where he was reading a newspaper at the kitchen table, and took off his glasses. "I'll help her get dressed," he said, smiling at Joy. "In fact, I'll go outside with them. Maybe we can build a snowman."

Piper gave a hoot of delight, and ran into the mudroom with the puppy bounding behind her.

"Thank you," Joy said gratefully. "I'll just finish up these cookies and then clean up and join you."

Eldon followed Piper into the mudroom, promising that their snowman would be the best snowman Glacier Creek had ever seen.

Beth smiled at Joy. "We had such a nice evening with Piper last night. She really is a treasure. Did you enjoy your date with Cole?"

Joy glanced suspiciously at the other woman. Beth continued stirring the fudge, but Joy wasn't fooled by her casual tone.

"It wasn't a date," Joy replied mildly. "He was just being nice, and thought I'd like to see a bit of the town."

Beth raised an eyebrow, but didn't contradict her. But as Joy arranged the cookies on a baking sheet, her thoughts returned to the previous evening.

He had kissed her.

True, it hadn't been much of a kiss, more a light brushing of his mouth across hers, but the contact had been so unexpected and quick she hadn't had time to react. Would she have kissed him back if he'd taken a little more time? She thought that perhaps she might have.

She had enjoyed dancing with Cole. He'd guided her through the steps with an easy confidence she found very attractive. With his height and his broad shoulders, he'd made her feel feminine and fragile in a way she hadn't felt since Matt had been alive. And the way he'd looked at her…

"What are you smiling at?" Beth asked, interrupting her thoughts. "As if I can't guess."

With a sense of surprise, Joy realized she *was* smiling, and warm color wash into her face.

"I was just thinking how wonderful it is to be here," she replied, which wasn't entirely untrue.

"It's been wonderful for us, too," Beth said, looking out the kitchen window to where Piper and Eldon were building a snowman, while Montana snuffled his face in the snow, his tail wagging happily. "I haven't seen Eldon this happy in—" She broke off. "Well, in a long time."

"Can I ask you a personal question?" Joy asked. "Why are there no pictures of Matt or Piper in the house?"

Beth poured the hot fudge mixture into a pan, and for a moment she didn't answer. When she finally looked at Joy, her expression was sad.

"These past few years have been hard for both Eldon and myself, but especially difficult for Eldon," she said. "He packed the photos away because they were just too painful to see every day."

"I understand," Joy replied. But she didn't.

"Having you both here has been like a breath of fresh air," Beth continued. "The house has been too quiet, for too long. Piper and that puppy—" She laughed. "Well, it's been the perfect remedy."

They finished baking the rest of the cookies, and Joy was just wiping down the countertops while Beth washed the last of the pans, when the mudroom door opened and Piper and Montana burst in, bringing a rush of cold air with them.

"Mommy, come see our snowman!" she cried. "It's bigger than me!"

Leaning to look out the window, Joy saw Eldon standing next to a snowman that was at least a foot taller than Piper. They had broken off some sticks for his arms, and had pushed some small rocks into his face to form eyes and a smiling mouth.

"He's wonderful," Joy said, impressed by their handiwork.

"Grampy sent me inside to get a carrot for his nose," Piper declared. "Then we're going back to see the festibul!"

"That sounds like fun!" Beth handed her a long carrot, and then pulled a spare woolen scarf from one of the hooks in the mudroom. "Here," she said. "We don't want your snowman to catch a cold!"

"Grammy, snowmen can't catch colds," Piper said, laughing. "They *are* cold!"

After the snowman had been completed, and Montana had been placed in his crate, they all drove back into town to see the rest of the festival.

Joy didn't know who had been more surprised—her or Beth—when Eldon had suggested they go to the festival. But they had quickly donned their boots and coats before he could change his mind.

Since it was a Saturday, the festival was even more crowded than it had been the day before. A petting zoo had been set up on the common, next to Santa's Village. Santa wasn't in yet, but they stopped at the petting zoo so Piper could feed the sheep and the goats, and take a ride on a small pony.

Joy and Beth watched as a handler led the pony around a small corral, while Eldon walked beside Piper, his hand hovering at the small of her back in case she should fall.

"He loves this," Beth murmured, as Piper said something to him, making him laugh.

"I'm sorry we haven't been to visit more often," Joy replied. "That wasn't fair to you, or to Piper. She loves Montana, and I'm not talking about the puppy."

"Well, you're here now," Beth said, and linked her arm through Joy's, giving her a small squeeze.

When Piper was finished with her pony ride, they meandered their way through the festival, stopping to buy a small bag of warm, candied nuts at one booth, and a pretty snowflake ornament at another. Piper walked beside her grandfather, hanging on to his hand and peppering him with questions. Then, without warning, she broke free from Eldon's hand and darted across the street.

"Piper!" Joy shouted, and ran after her. There were no cars permitted on the street during the festival, so she wasn't nervous about that, but with so many people, she was afraid she'd lose sight of her daughter.

She came to a stop at a large white tent, hung with a banner that read *Christmas Trees* and, under that, *Glacier Creek Forest Service*. Beside the tent stood a Christmas tree lot with row after row of trees alongside a display of wreaths and garlands, all arranged under strings of white lights. Piper had spied Cole, who was working the lot, and had launched herself into his arms.

Now he held the little girl, even as his eyes scanned the crowd and found Joy.

"Piper!" she said, reaching for her daughter. "You cannot just run away from us like that! What if something had happened to you?"

"I saw Mr. Tanner," she said, as if that explained everything, and to a certain extent, it did.

Joy tried not to notice how handsome he looked today. He hadn't shaved, and the shadow of beard growth on his square jaw made her want to rub her fingers across it just to feel the texture.

"I'm sorry," she said to Cole, setting Piper down. "She saw you from across the street, and she was gone before I could stop her."

"That's alright," he said, giving Piper a solemn wink. "She was just telling me about Montana, and the snowman she made this morning."

Beth and Eldon had caught up with them, and Eldon confirmed that the snowman was, indeed, the best snowman in Glacier Creek, and maybe even in Montana. Joy took the opportunity to covertly study Cole. He wore a heavy wool jacket in a red and black buffalo plaid over a denim shirt. He grinned broadly at something Piper said, and Joy's breath caught in her chest.

Why did he have to be so handsome?

As if sensing her examination of him, he looked at her, and his smile changed, became more personal. Joy blushed.

"How long are you working the tree lot, son?" Eldon asked. "I thought I'd take the ladies over to the diner for lunch. Maybe you could join us."

"I'd like that," Cole said, "but right now I don't have anyone to cover my shift."

"Do you sell Christmas trees?" Piper asked, her small face expressing puzzlement.

"Today I do," Cole confirmed. "Every time I sell a tree, some of the money gets used to buy boots and hats for the firefighters."

"Why don't you bring a tree home to decorate?" she asked innocently, shrugging her shoulders. "You said you don't have time to shop for one, but maybe you can take one of these ones."

Cole had the grace to look embarrassed, but when he cast a helpless glance in Joy's direction, she just arched an eyebrow in question. Piper had a good point, and there was no reason why Cole—and Eldon—couldn't bring a tree home.

"Well," he said carefully, looking at Piper, "I can't bring one of these trees home, because I have to sell these."

"But can't you just buy one?" Piper asked.

"Maybe he doesn't have any money," Joy said in a half-whisper, winking at her daughter.

Cole gave Joy a tolerant look, before crouching down in front of Piper. "Because I'd rather go into the woods and find a Christmas tree," he said. "There's something special about discovering the perfect tree, still covered in snow and pinecones, and bringing it home. I just haven't found the right tree yet, so I guess I'll need to keep looking."

Piper frowned, and Joy could almost see the wheels turning in her head as she geared up to ask Cole yet another question. Before she could say anything, however, a man strode up to the tent and slapped Cole on the back.

"Hey, man," he said, as the two men shook hands. "What are you doing here? The toboggan races are about to begin."

The other man was about Cole's age, no more than thirty or so. Beneath his brimmed hat, he wore his dark blonde hair pulled back into a ponytail, and he sported a neat beard.

Cole turned to Joy. "Meet my good friend, Dylan McCafferty. Dylan is one of the career firefighters here in Glacier Creek. Dylan, this is Joy Holliday and her daughter, Piper."

Joy saw the recognition in Dylan's eyes as he swept his hat from his head and shook Joy's hand. "A pleasure, ma'am. I would have known who you are just by looking at your little girl."

Piper was looking from one adult to the other, clearly not following the discussion. Joy was just as glad.

"Do you normally participate in the toboggan races?" she

asked, steering the conversation back to safer ground.

"Cole is the local tobogganing champion," Dylan said. "In the last ten years, he's never been beaten in his category."

"Wow," she said, suitably impressed, but unable to suppress a grin. "I guess now I know what you do in the winter! How else could you achieve such a lofty accomplishment?"

Cole narrowed his eyes at her while Beth and Eldon laughed. "Go ahead and mock me, but I promise you it's not as easy as it sounds. Tobogganing takes real skill."

"Tell you what," Dylan interjected. "I'll stay here and man the tent. Why don't you and Joy enter the tobogganing contest together?"

Joy looked at him in horror. "Oh, no. That's quite all right."

Cole exchanged a knowing look with Dylan. "She's from California. She's never been on a toboggan before, so don't judge her for being scared."

Piper chortled with delight. "Mommy, they said you're scared of a tob—a toggob—"

"A toboggan," Joy supplied helpfully.

"What *is* a toboggan?" Piper asked.

"It's just a sled, no big deal."

"No big deal?" Cole said in disbelief. "Ms. Holliday, would you do me the honor of being my partner in the toboggan races?"

"Oh, no—" Joy protested.

"Yes, yes, Mommy!" Piper yelled, jumping up and down and clapping her hands.

"We'll take Piper with us and watch from the top of the

run," Beth said, her eyes sparkling with amusement. "Go ahead. You'll have fun."

"We'll meet you at the diner afterwards," Eldon said. "Piper will be getting hungry and cold, so we'll head over right after the race and save a table."

"It's all set, then," Cole confirmed, and caught Joy by the hand. "We'd better hurry if we want to register and get a sled before the race starts."

Within ten minutes, Joy found herself seated on the back of a long wooden sled, at the top of a steep, seemingly endless mountain. Cole called it a hill, but Joy was pretty sure it was a mountain.

"Okay back there?" he asked.

They teetered on the edge of the summit, and the first two feet of the toboggan hung out over the precipice. Cole had his feet planted in the snow to keep them from plummeting downward.

"I think so," she answered, hoping he didn't notice the quaver in her voice.

Both she and Cole had been provided with safety helmets and goggles, and now Joy wondered just what she had gotten herself into.

"Put your legs over mine, and wrap your arms around me," Cole instructed. "Follow my lead, and just do what I do. Lean with me when I lean, even if you think we're going to wipe out."

"Okay, you're completely freaking me out," Joy said to him, but obediently scooted forward enough to place her boots alongside Cole's legs, keeping her heels on the wooden sled. He surprised her by lifting her legs and placing them firmly over his thighs, so that her feet were tucked between his knees.

"Hold onto me," he said.

Joy did.

She should have felt embarrassed with her arms wrapped around his waist and her legs curled over his, but instead she inched even closer.

"Here we go!" he shouted, and rocked them forward, lifting his feet onto the sled and pushing them over the edge.

Then they were flying, airborne, down the hill. Joy shrieked and clung to Cole, feeling both terrified and thrilled beyond words. She tried to remember his instructions to lean with him when he leaned. From her peripheral vision, she was vaguely aware of the many spectators along the race route, shouting encouragement as they whizzed past. They hit a bump and the toboggan lurched to one side. Joy screamed again and clung to Cole, barely resisting the urge to put her feet out and slow them down.

They continued to accelerate as they whooshed down the hill, and Joy laughed with delight, until she realized they were rapidly approaching the bottom, and a dense line of trees. Joy's eyes widened. Someone had placed a row of hay bales at the end of the toboggan run, but they looked woefully inadequate to stop their flight.

As the finish line drew near, she was certain they would crash into the trees. Without conscious thought, she stuck one foot out, dragging her booted heel through the snow. Instantly, the toboggan flipped onto its side, spilling both

Joy and Cole into the snow where they tumbled over each other, and finally came to a stop in a tangled heap.

Joy lay half-sprawled across Cole's body with snow on her face, in her mouth, and wedged into the openings of her helmet. Her goggles were gone completely. She laughed helplessly. Cole managed to sit up, and pulled her to a sitting position beside him.

"Are you okay?" he asked, pushing his goggles onto the top of his helmet. "Are you hurt?"

Joy shook her head and swiped the snow from her face. "No," she finally managed, breathless with laughter. "I'm fine!"

Cole removed his helmet, and his thick hair stuck up in all directions, making her want to giggle even more. In the bright sunlight, his eyes were incredibly blue. She could see the striations of color in his irises, and the tiny scar on his square jaw. He was covered in snow and without thinking, she reached out to brush if from his coat.

"That was amazing!" she said, grinning at him. "Do you think we won?"

Cole began to laugh. He pulled her close and gave her a hug, before he bracketed her face in his big, gloved hands.

"Darlin'" he said, "In fifteen years, I've never, ever lost the toboggan race, but in less than two minutes you managed to decimate my perfect record."

"How do you know?" Joy asked.

He grinned. "Because we never even made it across the finish line!"

And then he kissed her—a real kiss, warm and hungry,

and so heady that Joy was helpless to resist. At the first touch of his mouth against her, something ignited inside her; something hot and needy. She kissed him back, sliding her arms around his neck and reveling in the taste and feel of him. When his tongue pressed sensuously against hers, she opened to accept him, feeling a response bloom low in her center. When he finally pulled back, neither of them was laughing anymore. They stared at each other for a long moment, and then Cole smiled and lowered his forehead to hers.

"I never knew losing could feel so damned good."

Joy couldn't agree more.

Chapter Eight

COLE JOINED THEM for lunch at Red's Diner, where Eldon and Beth had secured a booth. Cole seemed to know everyone in the place, and accepted the friendly ribbing about losing his champion title with good grace, promising a comeback the following year.

"If you want to be my toboggan partner again," he said in a low aside to Joy, "you're going to need to practice. That means spending a whole lot more time out here in Glacier Creek, where there's plenty of snow and sledding."

Joy glanced at him to see if he was serious or just kidding but he'd shifted his attention to Piper, who was showing him just how much of the menu she could read by herself. Joy took the opportunity to study him. With his square jaw and chiseled cheekbones, some might call him hard, but his mouth was wide and mobile, and she knew firsthand just how warm and gentle it could be. She thought again of the kiss on the snowy hillside, and reflexively touched her fingers to her own lips. The kiss had been as hot as it had been unexpected.

As if sensing the direction of her thoughts, Cole slid his gaze to hers, and held it for a second longer than necessary, letting her know that he, too, was thinking about that kiss.

Flustered, Joy gave Piper a bright smile and pretended to study the menu with her, when in reality she wasn't capable of seeing or comprehending a single word of what was written there.

After a lunch of warm soup and grilled cheese sandwiches, they ventured back to the festival, where Eldon bought Piper a funnel cake, and then ended up having to eat most of it himself.

"Mmm," he said appreciatively, between bites. "I haven't had one of these in years. Almost forgot how tasty they are!"

The sun was dipping behind the mountains and casting long shadows over the town by the time they decided to head home. As they made their way back to the car, the overhead festival lights blinked on, causing Piper to gasp in delight.

They were just passing the center of the common, where Santa's Village stood. There, in front of the brightly lit tree, sat the jolly old elf himself, flanked by two elves who were handing out chocolate dipped candy canes.

"Mommy," Piper said, pulling on Joy's hand until she was forced to stop. "Look! There's Santa!"

"I see," she said, exchanging a smile with Beth.

"I think it's really him," Piper continued, her voice excited and awed. "Not one of his helpers."

Joy had to admit the town had hired a very realistic-looking Santa. From where she stood, his beard looked authentic, and even his round belly appeared to be his own, and not fake padding. The line of children waiting to see Santa wasn't too long, so when Piper asked if she could sit on his lap, Joy agreed.

"I'll wait in line with you," Cole offered.

"What are you going to say to him?" Joy asked Piper, as they drew closer to Santa.

"I can't tell you," Piper said, very seriously. "That's between me and Santa." She tipped her head back and looked up at Joy. "But I am going to make sure he knows I'm staying with Grammy and Grampy."

Cole laughed out loud. "I'm sure he already knows, pipsqueak."

Then it was Piper's turn. Cole and Joy stepped to one side and watched as Santa beckoned her forward. Even up close, he looked like the real deal. He lifted Piper onto his knee, and when Piper showed signs of being too shy to speak to him, Santa bent his head so that she could whisper in his ear. He listened, and then lifted his head and looked at Joy and Cole, and Joy could have sworn his eyes twinkled. He said something to Piper in a low voice, and the little girl threw her arms around him in an impulsive hug, before accepting a candy cane and climbing down.

"What did he say to you?" Joy asked when they rejoined Beth and Eldon and continued walking.

"He said this will be my best Christmas ever!" She slipped one hand into Joy's and the other into Cole's, skipping between them with a satisfied smile on her face.

Joy exchanged looks with Cole. He knew what had been on Piper's Christmas list, and he knew that two of her three wishes had already been fulfilled. With Christmas just four days away, and Cole the only single guy in their small circle,

Joy wondered if Piper thought Cole might somehow fit the bill for a new father. Joy wanted to reassure him she had no intention of setting her sights on him as a potential husband or new daddy for her daughter, no matter how attractive she found him. But she didn't dare say anything for fear Piper would discover she had opened her letter to Santa.

"Did he say anything else?" Cole asked.

"He didn't have to," Piper said confidently. "He already knows what I want for Christmas."

"Oh, sweetie," Joy began, "I'm not sure he can really bring you *everything* you want. He's just one of Santa's helpers."

"No, he was Santa," Piper insisted. "The *real* Santa!"

Pulling her hands free from their grasp, she went to walk with her grandparents, instead.

"Did you recognize the man who was in the Santa suit?" Joy asked Cole. "Is he a local? Maybe it would be better if Piper could see him out of his costume, so she doesn't get her hopes up too much."

"I've never seen him before," Cole replied. "He may have been hired from out of town. But I wouldn't worry too much. There's nothing wrong with Piper believing in Santa. I hope she keeps that innocence for a long time."

He was right, but Joy couldn't quite shake her concern that Piper might actually expect to find a new daddy waiting for her on Christmas morning.

AFTER THEY RETURNED to the house, Cole left to take care of Lucy and the puppies, but agreed to come back and have dinner with them. Piper was exhausted, but the little girl was so excited about her meeting with Santa, she refused to take even a short nap.

"We need to decorate the house!" she insisted. "Santa will be here in *four* days!" She threw her little hands up in exasperation. "We don't even have a Christmas tree!"

"You're right," Joy agreed. "But if you agree to take a nap, then first thing tomorrow we'll go into the attic and see what Grammy has for decorations."

"Today?" Piper pleaded, looking at Joy with her best puppy eyes. Beside her, Montana gave a little yip, and then flopped on the floor with his legs stretched out behind him, and laid his head on his front paws.

"Tomorrow," Joy repeated firmly. "See? Even Montana is tired."

Eldon entered the room with a mug of coffee, and sat down on the couch near the fire. "Come here, darlin'," he said to Piper. "Come sit next to your old Grampy, and I'll tell you a story."

"About Santa Claus?" she asked hopefully.

Eldon patted the cushion beside him. "Yes, about Santa. And about a little boy who thought he could stay awake all night and catch Santa as he came down the chimney."

"My daddy?"

Eldon nodded and Piper was hooked. Climbing onto the couch, she curled up next to her grandfather, and then coaxed the puppy up, too. Joy made herself comfortable in one of the roomy leather club chairs and listened as Eldon related the story. She'd heard it before, of course, but he had a way of bringing it to life every time he told it. Soon, Piper's head lolled against his arm and her eyelids grew heavy. Eldon made her comfortable, never missing a beat in telling the story. When her eyes closed and her mouth grew slack, Eldon eased a throw pillow beneath her head, and tenderly smoothed the bright, wayward curls from her face. Montana yawned and shifted closer to Piper, curling up against her legs.

Eldon stood up slowly so as not to disturb the sleeping duo, and gave Joy a slow wink. "It works every time," he said softly.

Joy stood up and gave him a hug. As many times as he told that particular story about Matt, it never failed to make him a little sad.

"Are you okay?" she asked, pulling back to look at him.

"I am," he said, and looked at Piper. "I am more than okay."

Joy smiled. "She adores you."

He made a harrumphing sound, and pressed a kiss against her forehead. "I have some work to do before dinner."

Joy watched him leave the room, and then spread a light throw over Piper, before going into the kitchen to help Beth with the meal. When Cole arrived two hours later, a fragrant stew simmered on the stove, and two loaves of homemade bread sat cooling on the counter.

The scent of the cold, night air still clung to him as he

entered the house. He was so big and handsome and vital, that Joy found herself pausing in the act of setting the dinner table just to watch him. He'd changed his clothes, and now he wore a dark gray Henley, open at the throat and pushed up over his strong forearms. He gave Beth a kiss on the cheek, and then looked over at Joy. He didn't say anything, but the expression in his eyes and the smile that lingered at the corners of his mouth made her feel as if he had just kissed her, too.

Blushing, she bent over her task, laying bowls and flatware at each place setting.

"Mmm," he said, sniffing appreciatively. "Something smells amazing. Is that your beef stew, Beth?"

Beth smiled at him. "And Joy made homemade gingerbread for dessert. I told her it was your favorite."

Cole patted his flat stomach, drawing Joy's unwilling attention to his flat stomach and lean hips. "I'd better be careful or Piper is going to mistake *me* for Santa if I keep eating like this." He looked around. "Where is the pipsqueak, anyway? It's suspiciously quiet in this house, and when there's a five-year-old and a puppy in residence, that usually spells trouble."

Joy pulled her gaze away from him, wishing he didn't look so sexy. Wishing she didn't find him so incredibly appealing. "One would almost think you have experience in raising children."

"Nope, just in puppies, and I don't think there's much difference between the two. If there's trouble, they both manage to find it."

"She's asleep in the other room, but I should probably wake her up, or she'll never sleep tonight."

Cole followed her into the great room, where Piper was already stretching and rubbing her eyes. Seeing Cole, she pushed herself to a sitting position and gave him a toothless grin. Montana lifted his head and blinked sleepily, and then rose to his feet, whimpering with joy while his little tail wagged madly upon seeing Cole.

"Hey, pipsqueak," Cole said, reaching for the puppy. "Why don't I just take this little guy outside to do his business? Your Grammy might not let me stay for supper if he has an accident in the house, and I really don't want to miss the gingerbread your mom made."

He winked at Joy, and scooped the puppy up.

"C'mon, sweetie," Joy said after he left. "Let's get you washed up for supper."

"Mommy, do you like Mr. Tanner?" Piper asked as they made their way upstairs.

"Of course I like him," she said carefully. "Why do you ask?"

"Just wondering." Piper smiled. "I like him, too."

Joy washed her daughter's face, and tried to smooth out the tangles in the corkscrew curls. Where was this coming from, and did it have anything to do with her visit to Santa Claus? Joy smoothed her finger over Piper's freckled nose, and then planted a kiss on the tip.

"You know that when Christmas is over, we'll return home to California and Mr. Tanner will stay here in Glacier Creek, right?"

Piper shrugged. "Maybe we could stay here, too."

"Honey, that's not possible."

"Why?"

Joy sighed. Piper was too young to understand that they couldn't just up and move to Montana, and Joy didn't want to get into a discussion about the one remaining item on the little girl's Christmas list. If Piper had any hope that Cole would step in to fill the empty place in both of their lives, Joy didn't want to be the one to crush her dreams.

Even if they were becoming her own dreams, too.

"Tell you what," she suggested, "let's go downstairs and have supper, and we'll talk about this tomorrow, okay?"

It was the coward's way out, but she hoped that by the following day, Piper would forget all about this conversation when something else captured her attention or imagination.

Dinner was festive and fun, as Cole repeated the story about the toboggan race and how Joy had managed to ruin his perfect record. He didn't mention the kiss, but from the way he looked at her, he was still thinking about it. She hated to admit she'd thought of little else all afternoon.

"I wondered if you and Piper would like to go ice-skating tomorrow," Cole said casually, breaking off a chunk of the homemade bread. "There'll be refreshments and hot chocolate, and some fun contests set up on the common, including a cow milking contest."

"With real cows?" Joy wasn't sure that sounded safe.

"Nah, it's a wooden cow with a rubber udder," Cole said with a laugh. "But it's still pretty fun for the kids."

Piper looked at her mother in hopeful anticipation. "Can

we, Mommy?"

"Of course. That sounds like fun."

"Great," Cole said, looking very satisfied, "I'll pick you up after lunch. Dress warm."

"Is there any other way?" Joy asked, laughing.

She would see Cole again tomorrow.

They had finished eating, and Cole had been extremely vocal in his praises of her gingerbread and homemade whipped cream. He had three helpings, groaning in exaggerated delight with each bite as Piper giggled uncontrollably.

"Why don't we have a game?" Eldon asked, as Joy and Beth cleared the table. His voice took on a mysterious quality, and he waggled his eyebrows at his granddaughter. "I have a board game that I think Piper will enjoy. Why don't we go sit in the other room by the fire?"

He pushed away from the table while Joy and Beth exchanged a questioning look.

"I really have no idea what he's up to," Beth admitted. "But I'm not about to question it!"

Cole scooped Piper from her chair and carried her, squealing, beneath his arm like a sack of potatoes. "C'mon, pipsqueak," he said, "let's go hosey the best seats."

"Careful," Joy warned as Piper laughed. "She just ate!"

"Ah," he said, setting her on her feet. "Kids really are like puppies!"

As Eldon stoked the fire, Beth made a bowl of popcorn and they all sat around the large, low coffee table. Eldon set a colorful box onto the table and explained the rules. Only there were no rules, just a series of cards that contained two *would you rather* questions. Each player asked the person next to them the two questions, and that person had to choose the least objective scenario. After several hilarious rounds, Joy's cheeks ached from laughing.

Now Piper held a card, and with Grammy's help, read it to Cole, unable to contain her grin. "Would you rather be bald all over, or hairy all over?"

Cole pretended to consider. "Well, being bald all over would sure save me some time shaving in the morning." He deliberately stroked his jaw, where clearly he hadn't shaved in a day or two. "But Montana gets mighty cold in the winter, so I'll have to go with... being hairy all over!"

He pretended to be a giant, hairy bear and raised his paws at Piper, who screamed in mock terror and fell over, while Montana leaped on her, barking.

"Okay, it's your turn," Joy said to Cole, when another round of cards had been read.

Cole drew a card, read it silently, and then looked meaningfully at Joy. "I want you to think carefully before you answer this one."

"Read it!" Piper demanded, laughing, and furtively fed the puppy another kernel of popcorn.

"Okay, here goes." He cleared his throat. "Would you, Joy Holliday, rather be... sweaty all the time, or have a hairy tongue?"

"Ew!" Joy and Piper exclaimed at the same time.

"C'mon, you have to choose," Cole said.

"That's not much of a choice," Joy complained. She looked at Beth. "What would you do?"

Beth ruffled Piper's hair. "I sometimes think I've had enough of the cold here in Montana, so if I could be sweaty in say, Hawaii, that's what I would choose."

"What would you choose?" Joy asked Piper.

"Hey, no fair," Cole protested. "This isn't a game where you get a lifeline, or help from a friend. You have to make your own choices."

Joy gave Piper a big smile. "Well, we're partners in crime, so whatever decisions I make, I make with her."

Piper grinned back at her. "I would choose a hairy tongue!"

Cole made an expression of disgust. "Okay, I have to ask why you would choose that."

Piper giggled. "Because if I got lonely, I could pet it, like I do Montana!"

Even Grampy laughed out loud, and Joy gave Piper a swift hug. The evening had been filled with laughter, and for the first time since she lost Matt, she was happy. Really, truly happy.

"I hate to be a party-pooper, but think it's time for little girls to be in bed," Beth announced.

Eldon looked at his watch. "Well my goodness, it is getting late."

Piper groaned loudly. "Nooo… Please can I stay up late?"

Joy laughed. "It is late, pumpkin. Grammy's right—it's time for bed."

"C'mon, pipsqueak," Cole said, standing up. "I'll carry you upstairs."

Piper jumped up, but she was unprepared when Cole turned her upside down and carried her feet first, screaming with laughter, up the stairs. Joy followed, knowing this was what Piper had been missing—the closeness of family, and a male figure who would make her feel special and loved.

Cole deposited her on the lower bunk in the guest room, across the hallway from Joy's bedroom, and then turned on the bedside lamp.

"This is where I used to sleep," he told Piper. "If you look close, you can see my initials carved into the wood over your head."

"Mommy won't let me sleep on the top bunk," she said.

"Probably a good idea, because then Montana wouldn't be able to sleep with you."

The puppy had followed them up the stairs, and now Cole lifted him onto the bed where he whined happily and slathered Piper's face with kisses.

Cole tweaked the little girl's nose. "Sleep tight, Pip-squeak. I'll see you tomorrow."

"Thank you," Joy said, as he stepped into the hallway. "This was a wonderful day for Piper. You're not leaving right away, are you?"

"I'll be downstairs."

After tucking her daughter into bed, Joy went down to find Cole sitting by the fire talking quietly with Eldon and Beth. Beth sat in one of the leather club chairs with a basket of yarn at her feet, knitting what looked like a deep blue sweater. With no other option, Joy sat down on the sofa next to Cole. She tried to focus on the conversation, but all she could think about was how his jeans hugged the muscular contours of his thighs, and how much she liked listening to the deep timber of his voice as he talked. He held a tumbler of bourbon in his hands, and the liquid glowed dark amber in the firelight. His hands were strong… a working man's hands, but they were also capable of gentleness. What would those hands feel like on her skin?

The conversation continued, and then turned to discussions about the timber mill, and an order that Cole hoped to fill right after the holiday. Soon, the fire was little more than a bed of glowing coals in the grate, and Joy grew drowsy. She had slipped sideways on the deep sofa, and now her arm pressed against Cole's.

"Well," Eldon said, rising to his feet, "I think we'll go ahead and turn in."

Setting aside her knitting, Beth stood up. Cole half rose to his feet, but she waved him back. "You stay as long as you'd like, Cole. This is your home, too, and you don't need to rush out. I'm sure Joy would enjoy the company."

They said good night, and then it was just Joy and Cole, alone on the sofa. They sat in silence for several minutes, until Cole rubbed his hands over the top of his thighs. "It's getting pretty late," he finally said. "You look about done in, so I think I'll get going."

If Joy didn't know better, she'd think he was actually nervous. He stood up, and extended a hand to her. She took it, letting him tug her to her feet. She was tired, but also reluctant to see what had been a magical day come to an end.

"I'll walk you out," she murmured.

She waited as he pulled on his heavy shearling jacket, and retrieved his hat from the hook.

"Thanks for letting me spend some time with you and Piper today," he said, turning the hat in his hands. "Sometimes it's nice to see the world through a child's eyes."

"It was nice seeing Glacier Creek through your eyes," Joy countered.

Settling his hat on his head, Cole opened the door. Snow had begun to fall, drifting down in soft, fat flakes.

"Oh, how pretty!" Joy exclaimed.

"It looks pretty now," Cole said, "but we'll have another foot or more by tomorrow night."

"Maybe we should postpone our outing," Joy suggested. "I don't want to risk having an accident if the roads are going to be bad."

Cole turned and smiled at her, and something shifted in Joy's chest.

"We'll be fine," he assured her. He put his hand on the door handle. "You should go inside before you get cold."

Joy looked past him to the dark forest that surrounded the house, and she could sense how reluctant he was to return to his own empty house.

"I'm sure Lucy and the puppies will be happy to see you," she said. "Drive safely." She started to close the door and then, before she could chicken out, she leaned up and pressed a kiss against his lips. "Thank you again for today."

"Ah, damn," he muttered softly, and then he slid one hand to the back of her head and lowered his mouth to hers.

This time, his kiss was slow and deliberate. His mouth

was warm and firm as it explored hers, tasting her until she finally leaned into him and returned the kiss, welcoming the intrusion of his tongue against hers. She hadn't known a kiss could be so potent, causing her heart rate to accelerate and her blood to heat. When he finally pulled back, she thought she might actually melt, like the little snowflakes that landed on his skin and became tiny beads of moisture.

"Woman," he growled softly, "you are dangerous."

She *felt* dangerous. She felt powerful.

The smolder in his blue eyes made her feel sexy and reckless. He made her feel beautiful and *alive*.

She pushed her hands inside the opening of his heavy coat and wrapped her arms around him, reveling in his warmth. His muscles bunched beneath her fingertips as she stroked them across his back, exploring the contours of his spine. He was hard everywhere and she ached to know what he looked like beneath the heavy shirt. She guessed he would be layered with muscle. Just thinking about it caused moist heat to gather at her center and blossom outward. She'd almost forgotten what desire felt like.

"You feel so good," she murmured, and pressed her lips against the pulse that beat strongly at the base of his throat. "You smell good, too."

He gave a soft groan and tipped her face up, claiming her mouth in kiss so hot, Joy half-expected steam to rise from her skin. This time, when he broke the kiss, he bent his head to hers, and his breathing sounded ragged.

"Baby, I have to go now, or I may not go at all." His voice was a rough rasp.

"I'll see you tomorrow?" Her voice sounded breathless.

She forced herself to pull away, but used the excuse of buttoning his jacket as a reason to keep touching him.

"I'm counting on it," he said. "Good night, darlin'." He tipped his hat to her, before striding to his truck.

Joy closed the door, and watched through the glass as he reversed out of the circular drive and disappeared into the darkness. Slowly, she made her way upstairs, shutting off the lights as she went.

She paused at Piper's door to look in on her. Piper was sound asleep, clutching her favorite yellow blankie. Joy smiled as she saw Montana curled up against the little girl, his nose tucked beneath Piper's chin.

The house was quiet as Joy climbed into her own bed, and she lay awake for a long time, thinking about Cole. He'd called her *baby* and *darlin'*. He'd made her ache for him in the best way possible—in a way she hadn't ached for any man in a long, long time. Even now, her body hummed with unfulfilled need.

Cole had wanted her, too. He'd made that clear. They'd only known each other for a few, short days, but there was a connection there. An attraction that couldn't be denied. It would be so easy to fall in love, completely and irrevocably, with Cole Tanner.

Joy turned on her side and bunched the pillow beneath her cheek. She'd always believed she would find love again in her lifetime. God couldn't be so cruel as to deny her that, not when she was only twenty-seven years old. Not when she was open to the possibility of a second chance at love.

But why would He be so cruel as to make her lose her heart to another wildland firefighter? Despite her growing feelings for Cole, she didn't know if she could let that happen. Because the risk of losing him was too great.

Chapter Nine

THE FOLLOWING MORNING was overcast and gray and, as Joy pulled her bathrobe on and looked out the window, she saw the snow was still coming down. But whereas the night before the snow had been light and fluffy, the flakes were now tiny and falling thick and fast. She peeked into Piper's room, but her bed was empty. She cocked her head and listened, but the house was quiet.

In the kitchen, Beth was just pulling a coffee cake out of the oven. She smiled when she saw Joy.

"Good morning. I'm glad you were able to sleep in a bit. I could see how tired you were last night."

"What time is it?"

"Almost nine o'clock."

"I'm so sorry—I never sleep past seven, mostly because Piper is such an early riser. I hope she didn't wake you up."

"Not at all, I was already awake when she and Montana came downstairs."

"Where are they now?" Joy pulled a mug down from the cupboard and poured herself some coffee. She remembered Cole's comment that when a five-year-old and a puppy were together, and the house was quiet, that usually spelled trouble. "I don't hear them."

Beth slid the coffee cake onto a cooling rack on the island, and removed her oven mitts. "I fed her a bowl of cereal, and took Montana out to do his business. That was over an hour ago. Eldon brought some toys down from the attic for her, so she's probably playing in his office while he works."

Uncertainty and something else niggled at the back of Joy's neck. She set her mug down on the counter. "I'll just go check."

She made her way through the great room, pausing to look at a pile of small toys in the middle of the room that looked like pieces to a play castle. There were tiny horses and colorful knights, along with dozens of plastic trees and animals, and miniature medieval furniture and weapons. On the coffee table, Piper had arranged a small forest of the trees and in the middle stood a tiny plastic princess and a gray wolf.

Eyeing the toys, Joy took the staircase that led to the lower lever, where Eldon had his office. She could hear the timber of Eldon's voice, but couldn't make out his words. Was he talking to Piper? As she turned the last corner on the stairs and his office came into view, her anxiety ratcheted up a notch. He sat at his big desk, talking on the phone. Blueprints and papers were spread out on his large drafting table, and the walls were covered in colorful print ads for his custom homes, as featured in some of Montana's top home and building magazines.

But there was no sign of Piper or the puppy.

Seeing her, Eldon lowered the phone. "What is it, dar-lin'?"

"Have you seen Piper? She's not in her room, and Beth thought she might be down here with you."

Eldon shook his head, his features creasing into a frown. "I left her in the great room with a bin of toys I dragged out of the attic. She's not there?"

"No. Maybe she's in the bathroom—I'll run upstairs and check again."

She took the stairs two at a time, calling Piper's name, but there was no answer. Beth came into the great room, her expression worried.

"She can't have gone far."

"Piper!" Joy shouted the little girl's name, but there was no response.

A sick feeling of dread settled into the pit of her stomach, and she eyed the snowstorm with anxiety as she ran up to the second level and searched all the bedrooms and bathrooms. Piper was nowhere to be found.

Dashing back downstairs, she stopped in the middle of the great room, where Eldon and Beth waited for her.

"I don't know where she is," she said. Her voice sounded high and panicky, even to her own ears. "I can't find her."

"Don't you fret," Eldon said soothingly. "We'll find her. Maybe she's hiding, thinking she'll have some fun with us."

"No, no," Joy shook her head. "That's not like Piper to do something like that."

Her gaze settled on the plastic toys, and the little princess surrounded by trees. She looked at Beth, stricken. "Are her coat and boots in the hallway?"

Piper's coat, hat, mittens, and boots were missing. Quickly, without changing out of her pajamas, Joy thrust her feet into her own boots and threw on her coat, while Beth and Eldon did the same.

"She may just be in the yard," Beth soothed. "Maybe she thought Montana needed to go out. I'm sure she's not far."

Joy prayed the older woman was right. But when they went outside, there was no sign of Piper or the puppy. The snow was falling so thick and fast Joy had to blink to keep it out of her eyes. She plowed through the snowdrifts until she had completely circled the house, while Eldon and Beth checked the nearby garage and shed. They met back at the door.

"She's gone!" Joy cried, and her voice broke. "She's nowhere!"

"I'll call Cole," Eldon said, and went back inside.

Beth put her arms around Joy. "We'll find her. We'll find her, and she's going to be fine. Please don't cry."

Joy didn't even know she *was* crying until Beth pulled off a mitten and wiped her face. Pulling away, Joy scanned the yard again, half expecting Piper to emerge from the surrounding trees with a triumphant laugh. But there was just silence and the falling snow.

A movement near the edge of the forest caught Joy's attention, and she peered through the snow to see what it was. There, near the dense tree line, a tiny hummingbird flashed bright green and red as it flitted about.

Joy began to walk toward it, expecting it would vanish at

any moment, but it continued to dart back and forth, hovering for a moment, and then flitting away. As she drew closer, Joy saw footprints beneath the tree boughs, where the falling snow hadn't yet filled them in. Small footprints, and beside them, the even smaller tracks of an animal. *Piper and Montana.*

Horror filled her as she realized that Piper had gone into the woods.

"She's here!" Joy shouted to Beth. "She went into the woods!"

Eldon returned outside, and together they entered the trees, shouting Piper's name. But the small footsteps were swiftly disappearing beneath the blowing snow, and tracking them became nearly impossible.

"Cole is on his way with Lucy," Eldon said. "Best we wait for them." He turned to his wife. "Go back to the house and let Cole know where we are, and then call the police. Tell them we have a missing child."

A missing child. Her child.

This couldn't be happening. Not to her.

Not to Piper.

This kind of horror happened to other people. It was the kind of thing one saw on the six o'clock news and thought, *thank God that isn't my child.*

Only it was.

Joy felt numb with fear. She couldn't even think about the consequences of not finding Piper; that place was too dark and too horrific to visit, even for an instant.

"We have to keep going," she said urgently to Eldon.

"We can't stop! She could be right up ahead. She must be so scared! Piper! Piper!"

"This is all my fault," Eldon said, his voice thick with emotion. "She wanted me to play with her this morning, but I thought getting a client's house plans finished was more important, so I brought down those toys from the attic for her to play with instead. If I'd just stayed with her—"

The sound of a dog barking made them turn, and Joy saw Cole striding through the trees, his long legs surging through the snow while Lucy bounded beside him. He wore a red ski parka and a knit hat pulled down over his head. He had a backpack on, and he carried a flashlight. His face was grim, and the sight of him destroyed the last vestiges of Joy's control.

"She's gone," she cried, and might have collapsed onto her knees, but Cole was there, supporting her.

"Listen to me," he said, and his voice brooked no argument. "We are going to find her. She's dressed warm, and she's been gone for less than an hour. Lucy will track Montana's scent, and we'll find them both. Do you understand me? We'll find her."

Joy nodded and tried to pull herself together, knowing she couldn't help Piper if she didn't stay calm. Cole gave her a brief, swift hug.

"Good girl."

He pulled something out of his backpack, and Joy saw it was Piper's yellow baby blanket, the one she slept with every night. He held it under Lucy's nose.

"Find her, girl. Find Piper."

The dog carefully sniffed the blanket, and then turned and began trotting through the snow, her nose down.

"Does she really know how to find them?" Joy asked.

She'd only ever seen a dog track someone in the movies. Lucy wasn't a trained police dog. How could they trust her enough to follow her?

"That blanket has the scent of both Piper and the puppy on it," Cole said. "Lucy has an exceptional nose. She'll find them."

The three of them followed the dog, and Joy fretted as the terrain became steeper. How could a five-year-old possibly have come this far? The snow was too deep; she never would have ventured this far into the woods, not when the snowdrifts must be up to her thighs. What possible reason could she have had to wander so far away from the house?

They each shouted Piper's name, over and over, but there was no answer. What if they were wrong? What if she'd gone in another direction? With each step, Joy became more convinced they were wasting precious minutes searching in the wrong area.

"Cole—" she began.

"Shh!" He stopped and held up a hand to forestall her words. "Did you hear that?"

Joy and Eldon stopped, and at first Joy didn't hear anything, but then Lucy gave a series of barks and her tail began to wag. That's when Joy heard a small, frantic bark in return.

"That's Montana!" she exclaimed.

"Damned right," Cole said. "C'mon, Lucy, go get her!"

They began to run after the dog, hampered by the deep snow, until they came to top of a ridge. Lucy stood at the edge, barking wildly. There, at the bottom of a steep ravine, lay Piper. Montana stood beside her, his entire body wriggling with excitement as he barked uncontrollably.

Joy's heart stopped as she saw Piper's motionless form. Only her red knit hat was visible, where Montana had been lying with his head on top of hers. The rest of her was covered in a layer of snow.

Joy gave a distressed cry and leaped forward, ready to charge down the embankment, but Cole grabbed her and hauled her back.

"Wait here," he said. "I know you want to go to her, but it's steep and we don't need two accidents."

"Cole," she begged. "Please—"

Tipping his head down, he looked into her eyes. "Do you trust me?"

She stared at him, and then reluctantly nodded.

"Then stay here with Eldon. I'll bring her up."

COLE TIED A rope around a tree trunk, and used it to control his descent. Climbing to the bottom of the ravine was the hardest thing he had ever done, and it had nothing to do with the physical challenge of negotiating the steep embankment. He desperately needed for Piper to be alive, but she looked so small and still that his heart contracted painfully in his chest. He dreaded what he would find. If anything happened to Piper, it would completely destroy Joy.

It would destroy all of them.

"Please be okay, please be okay," he said beneath his breath, as he half leaped, half skidded down the steep incline, until finally, he was at the bottom of the ravine.

Montana whimpered in joy and leaped against him as Cole crouched beside the little girl. He used his teeth to pull his gloves from his hands, and spared the puppy one swift pat, before he gently turned Piper over. Her eyes were closed, her lips had started to turn blue, and her freckles stood out starkly against her pale skin. He pressed his fingers against the side of her throat and nearly wept with relief when he found a pulse.

"She's alive!" he shouted up to Joy and Eldon.

Joy collapsed against Eldon, and he heard the older man talking to her. Carefully, he began examining Piper for injuries, looking for a head wound or broken bones. But it wasn't until he ran his hands along her right arm that she cried out, and her eyelashes fluttered open. She stared at him in bemusement.

"Hey there, pipsqueak," he said, and smiled reassuringly at her.

"My arm hurts." She whimpered. "I fell down the hill."

"You're safe now, and I'm going to bring you home."

Cole could feel a suspicious lump in her forearm, and Piper whimpered when he probed the area. He was pretty sure the bone was broken, but it was difficult to tell through the winter coat.

"Okay, sweetheart, does it hurt anywhere else?"

"No."

Her teeth began to chatter uncontrollably. He needed to get her warm, and quickly. Swiftly, he pulled off his backpack and pulled out several hand-warmers and gave them a good shake to activate them. Then he pushed them inside Piper's coat, packing them all around her torso.

"Okay, pipsqueak, let's get you out of here."

"What about my puppy?"

Her speech was slow and slurred, sure signs of hypothermia. Cole scooped up the shivering puppy and placed him inside the backpack, on top of Piper's blanket, with only his head poking out the top. He put the pack on, and then lifted Piper in his arms, taking care not to jar her arm.

"Your puppy is just fine, and your mommy is waiting for you at the top of the hill," he said as he carefully made his way up the ravine, using the rope for balance and digging his boots into the snow as he tested each footstep. The going was slow, but then Eldon and Beth were reaching down to take Piper from him, so he could use his arms to pull himself the last several feet.

"Oh, baby, you had me so scared!" Joy was bent over Piper, raining kisses on her face.

"Careful of her right arm, it could be broken," Cole cautioned. "She's also suffering from hypothermia."

Eldon took the puppy out of the backpack and, as Lucy tried to lick the puppy's face, tucked Montana inside his heavy coat to keep him warm.

"Let's get her out of here," Cole said, and lifted Piper into his arms. Joy kept pace beside him, keeping one hand on Piper's leg as if she feared the little girl might vanish again.

Cole knew the danger of hypothermia, and he also knew that children lost heat from their bodies much faster than adults. Glancing down at her face, he saw Piper's eyes had closed again. He quickened his pace, not an easy task considering the depth of the snow.

"Hey, pipsqueak, can you open your eyes for me?" he asked.

She obediently opened her eyes, but Cole could see it was an effort for her. "I'm sleepy."

"Don't fall asleep, baby," Joy said, and Cole saw real fear in her eyes as she realized Piper might not yet be out of danger.

They were almost out of the woods when they were intercepted by two firefighters and two paramedics, each of them close friends of Cole.

"Thanks for the quick response," he said to the first man, Scott Ross. "I think she has a broken arm."

"We'll take care of her," Scott promised. "When the call came in, I think the entire base station wanted to respond."

Cole handed the child over to Scott, and then bent over with his hands braced on his knees for a moment to catch his breath. An ambulance and a fire rescue vehicle stood in the driveway, and Beth openly wept when she saw them emerge from the trees with Piper.

"I'll ride with her," Joy said, as they loaded the child into the back of the ambulance.

"We'll be right behind you," Cole promised.

They stood in the driveway and watched the two emergency vehicles depart through the falling snow, with lights on and sirens wailing.

Eldon pulled the puppy out from inside his coat, and cuddled the little dog against him for a moment, before looking at Cole.

"Thank you, son."

There was so much emotion in the older man's voice, and so much grief etched on his face, Cole went over and hugged him, and then pulled Beth into the embrace, too. He hadn't realized until that very moment just how much he had to be grateful for.

Chapter Ten

THEY ARRIVED AT the small hospital to learn that Piper did have a broken arm and mild hypothermia. They waited in the lobby area for almost an hour, before a doctor arrived.

Cole stood up as he recognized Dr. Sarah Sommerhoff, who frequently treated the firefighters when they came in with injuries. He stood up as she entered the small waiting area.

"How is she?" he asked without preamble. Behind him, Eldon and Beth stood up, clutching each other.

Sarah smiled. "She's going to be fine. The break in her arm has been set, and she's already doing much better. We're going to keep her overnight for observation, out of an abundance of caution, but I fully expect she'll be able to go home in the morning."

"Oh, thank goodness," Beth exclaimed. "May we see her?"

"Of course. We gave her a mild painkiller, so she's a little drowsy, but her mother is with her." Dr. Sommerhoff indicated the corridor behind her. "They're in Room 121."

Outside Piper's room, Cole waited while Eldon and Beth

went in first. He stood in the hallway for a moment, listening to the emotional reunion, and tried to harness his own rioting emotions. Even though the doc had assured him Piper would be fine, he couldn't get the image of her, lying so small and helpless at the bottom of the ravine, out of his head.

She could have died.

If they hadn't found her in time...

He swiped at his eyes and blew out a hard breath, unable to think about what might have happened.

"Hey. Are you okay?"

Joy stood in the doorway of Piper's room, looking at him with concern. He hadn't heard her approach. He summoned a smile.

"Yeah, I'm good. How are you doing?"

For the first time, he realized she was wearing her pajamas, and realized she must have dashed into the storm to look for Piper without even changing her clothes. She wore a pair of flannel lounge pants in a red and blue plaid, paired with a gray baseball shirt with blue sleeves. She wore no bra, and he could see the contours of her breasts beneath the material of the jersey. He hated that he noticed, especially now, but he couldn't help himself.

"I'm better now," she admitted. "Why are you standing out here? Piper has been asking for you."

"She has?"

Joy smiled. "Of course. You're her hero, you know. You saved her *and* her puppy."

"Jesus, Joy..." Just thinking about what might have happened nearly undid him, and he scrubbed a hand over his face.

"Hey," she said, and laid a hand on his arm. "You found her! Here's a newsflash; I was convinced we were wasting our time by following Lucy. I was two seconds away from telling you to turn around. If we'd done that—"

She broke off, and Cole saw the emotions that flashed across her face and threatened to crumple her composure. He pulled her into his arms, holding her tightly. She was trembling, and Cole felt a surge of protectiveness wash over him. He held her until she stopped shaking, and then set her gently away.

"Is she awake?"

Joy nodded and swiped her fingers across her damp cheeks. "Yes. I mean, just barely, but she's determined to stay awake until she sees you."

Piper sat propped up in bed with at least four pillows, as Eldon and Beth admired the neon pink cast that extended from her elbow to her fingers, and showered her with attention. She looked up as Cole entered, and broke into a smile.

"You came!"

He bent over the bedrail and tipped her face up. The color had returned to her lips and cheeks. Her pupils were huge from whatever painkiller they had administered, and she looked drowsy, but happy. He kissed her forehead.

"Of course I came, pipsqueak."

"Did you see my cast?" She yawned hugely.

"That's very... pink," he said, smiling. "You were very

brave."

"It hurted a lot, but not anymore." Her eyelids began to drift closed, but she opened them again, as if determined not to fall asleep.

"Let's go home, Eldon," Beth said to her husband. "We can come back tomorrow morning, when she's ready to be discharged. But she needs to sleep. The poor little thing can barely keep her eyes open."

Eldon made a harrumphing sound of displeasure, but he bent over the little girl and kissed her tenderly, before saying goodbye to Cole and Joy.

"I'll drive Joy home later," Cole assured them.

"Oh, but I'm not leaving. I'm planning to stay here, with Piper," Joy said. "The hospital staff is going to bring in a rollaway bed for me."

"Mind if I stay for a bit?" Cole asked. He was reluctant to leave. Eventually, he'd need to go home to let Lucy out and to feed both her and the pups but, for now, he just wanted to be with Joy and Piper.

They sat side by side next to the hospital bed, and Joy held her daughter's good hand. Piper drifted in and out of sleep, occasionally opening her eyes to see if they were still there, before relaxing again.

"I can't seem to let her go," Joy admitted to Cole. "If I could, I would just crawl into the bed with her and hug her tight."

Cole understood. He was feeling a little of that himself, where both of them were concerned. He just wanted to wrap his arms around Joy and keep her safe. In fact, he just flat out wanted to keep her. He wanted to keep them both. The revelation was both startling and alarming, since Joy would never agree to stay in Montana, especially not after today's events.

"Did she say why she went into the woods?" he asked quietly, as he watched Piper sleep.

"No. I didn't want to upset her by asking."

Piper cracked her eyes open, and her mouth curved upward in a sly smile. "I can hear you."

"You tricked us," Cole said, reaching out to tweak one of her toes beneath the blanket, eliciting a giggle. "Can you tell us why you went into the woods with Montana?"

Piper gave an enormous yawn. "To find a tree."

Cole frowned. "What do you mean?"

Joy leaned forward to protest, but Cole held up a finger. He needed to know.

"You said you had to go into the woods to find a perfect Christmas tree, so I wanted to help you," Piper said, looking anxious. "You don't have a Christmas tree, so I wanted to find one for you."

"Oh, Piper," Joy said softly, and leaned over the bed to hug her. "What a sweet, sweet thing to do."

Cole stared at the little girl, stricken. She had gone into the woods *for him*. Because he'd been too selfish and too wrapped up in his own bah-humbug to see that Piper didn't just want a perfect Christmas for herself—she wanted a perfect Christmas for everyone.

Even him.

"Piper," he began, and had to clear his throat. "That

might be the nicest thing anyone has ever done for me. But I don't ever want you to do something like that again. In future, promise me you'll bring an adult with you, okay?"

Piper nodded, but her lower lip trembled and her eyes welled. Cole felt like his heart might bust in half. He was mush. Complete and utter mush, and all because of a little girl's tears.

"No, don't cry," he said. "I'm not mad at you, pipsqueak, but I don't ever want to be scared the way I was scared today. If something happened to you, I could never forgive myself. Okay?"

"Okay," Piper whispered, and balled her fist against her eyes.

"Go to sleep, baby," Joy said softly, and leaned over to adjust Piper's pillows, and draw the blanket up more securely around her.

They sat in silence, watching her, until her eyes closed and her mouth went slack. Cole groaned and dropped his head into his hands.

"It wasn't your fault," Joy said, and she reached over to touch him.

"Don't try to make me feel better about this," he said, half lifting his head. "If I had just bought a damned tree from the lot that day, we wouldn't be spending the night at the hospital. When I think what might have happened—"

"Don't. She's safe because of you." Joy was quiet for a moment. "And because of a hummingbird."

Cole lifted his head and looked at her. "What?"

"While we were frantically searching around the house

for Piper, I saw a hummingbird at the edge of the forest," Joy said. "Honestly, it seemed to me as if it was trying to get my attention."

"Go on."

"As I approached it, that's when I saw Piper's footprints going into the forest. We didn't see any footprints in the yard because the snow was coming down so fast, they'd filled in. But these footprints were protected by the tree branches, so I could still see them." She looked earnestly at him. "But if I hadn't seen the hummingbird, I never would have spotted those tracks."

"Do you really believe the hummingbird was Matt, trying to send you a message?" He sounded skeptical, but he had a difficult time believing the tiny bird was a messenger, divine or otherwise.

"I don't know," Joy admitted. She leaned forward to gently stroke Piper's hair. "I only know that I believe in the possibility of miracles."

COLE STAYED WITH Piper and Joy through most of the afternoon, leaving only to bring back a small cooler from Beth with two home-cooked meals inside, along with a stuffed animal and a small bunch of balloons for Piper. He also had a stack of children's books, two recent bestseller mystery novels and some magazines for Joy.

"Something to pass the time for both of you," he explained.

He left soon after, explaining he had to meet with a couple traveling from Missoula to pick up one of the puppies, but he promised to come back and help Joy discharge Piper in the morning.

Despite her resolve not to lose her heart to Cole, Joy was sorry to see him go. She enjoyed his company, and his solid bulk was a comforting presence in the midst of doctors and nurses, and the smell of antiseptic and medicine. As evening approached, the staff brought in a small rollaway bed for her, and that night she curled up next to Piper and read the children's books to her, deeply grateful for the little girl's wriggly warmth and endless questions.

After Piper fell asleep, she pulled her rolling bed as close to Piper's as she could. She lay on her side looking at her child for a long time, before she finally fell asleep.

Cole arrived the next morning around nine o'clock. Doctor Sommerhoff had already made her rounds and had examined Piper and declared she could go home as soon as her discharge papers were ready. Beth had sent Joy a clean change of clothes, for which she was profoundly grateful. She didn't want to drive home in her pajamas.

"Did you get any sleep?" Cole asked after she had changed, looking closely at her.

Joy grimaced. "A little. But you know how hospitals are; they're forever coming in to check on you, so it's hard to get more than a few hours of sleep. But I didn't mind."

After the frightening events of the day, she'd been content to just lay awake, watching her daughter sleep.

Cole turned to Piper, who was busy packing her belongings into a bag that the hospital had provided for her. Joy had already dressed the little girl in her coat and hat. One sleeve hung empty, since Joy had insisted she wear the sling for her injured arm.

"What do you say, pipsqueak? Ready to go home?"

"Yes!"

Stepping into the hallway, he produced a wheelchair with an elaborate flourish. "Your chariot awaits!"

Piper's eyes rounded, and Joy could see she desperately wanted to ride in the wheeled chair, even though she didn't really need to.

"I can walk," she said, but her voice sounded uncertain.

"Ah, but it's a hospital rule that you be taken to your car in a wheelchair, so climb aboard."

Piper looked at Joy, who smiled and shrugged. "If it's the rule, then I guess you'll have to do it."

Cole carefully lifted her into the chair, as Piper smiled widely. He placed her new stuffed animal on her lap, while Joy carried her books and her balloons.

"Ready?" he asked.

She nodded, and they were off. Joy watched as Cole wheeled her through the hallways, going just a little bit faster than necessary. The two nurses on duty at the nursing station came around from behind the desk to wave goodbye to her.

"Goodbye!" Piper called, waving with her good hand. "Goodbye!"

Outside, the day was bright and cold, but Cole's truck sat at the curb and the cab was still warm. Joy watched as

Cole gently lifted Piper into the middle, where he had already installed her car seat. He adjusted the restraints so her arm was comfortable, and then helped Joy in beside her.

"Thank you," she said quietly, before he could shut the door. "For everything."

"It's my pleasure," he replied. "I mean that sincerely."

He held her gaze for several long seconds, until Joy felt her face turn warm beneath his regard. Smiling at her, he closed the door.

"I bet Montana missed me," Piper said as they drove through town.

"I'm sure he did," Joy said. "He'll be very happy to see you again."

Piper laughed. "Yeah, he's going to be so wiggly!" Then her voice grew despondent. "But I won't be able to pick him up."

"Not right away you won't," Cole agreed. "But he'll be happy just being with you, even if you can't carry him around. He's getting too big for that, anyway. You don't want to spoil him too much."

They turned onto the road that led to Eldon and Beth's. Snow lay heavily on the tree branches and on the road, and sparkled like diamonds beneath the bright sun. They passed the long drive that led to Cole's house, and were soon turning onto the private road that led to Eldon and Beth's house. There were a number of SUVs and pickup trucks parked along the length of the long driveway, and Joy looked over at Cole.

"What's going on? Why are there so many cars here?"

Cole just gave her a smile and then winked at Piper. As the trees cleared, and the timber frame house came into view, both Joy and Piper gave a gasp of astonishment. The entire house had been trimmed in bright Christmas lights. An enormous wreath, at least nine feet across, hung on the side of the house. Thick, green swags of evergreen, fortified with white lights and large silver balls, hung over the doorways and wound around the light poles. Even the nearby trees and shrubs had been strung with lights. On the snowy lawn stood an old-fashioned sleigh, and in the back stood a fully decorated Christmas tree.

At least a dozen people stood in front of the house, and they each began to clap as Cole parked the truck and turned off the engine. Joy recognized Scott Ross and Tyler Dodson, and guessed the others must also be Cole's buddies from the fire station. As Cole climbed down from the truck, Beth and Eldon came forward to open Joy's door, both of them wearing red Santa hats.

Joy looked over at Piper, who stared at the house in wonder, her good hand clapped over her mouth.

"Grampy!" she exclaimed, as Joy unfastened her seat belt and Eldon reached in to lift her out. "You finally decorated your house for Christmas!"

"For you, Piper," he said gruffly, kissing her face. "We decorated it for you."

Chapter Eleven

ELDON CARRIED PIPER toward the house for a better look, and Beth hovered by her side, ready to bring her indoors at the first sign of exhaustion or pain.

Cole came to stand next to Joy as they watched Piper. "She deserves this. We should have done this long before you arrived in Montana."

Impulsively, Joy hugged him. "Thank you so much. You must have worked all night to pull this off."

"Well, I had some help."

He introduced Joy to the rest of the firefighting crew, and then invited them all inside for a cup of coffee and some of Beth's homemade coffee cake.

As Joy entered the house, she stopped, and this time she was the one who put her hands over her mouth in awe. If the men had done a great job decorating the outside of the house, the women had done an even more spectacular job on the inside.

Garlands and wreaths hung from the beams and the walls, and tiny bunches of mistletoe had been placed in each doorway. A Christmas tree stood in one corner of the kitchen, and through the doorway to the great room, Joy saw a second tree in front of the soaring windows, and the stone fireplace had been decorated with fresh greens. The entire house looked as if it belonged in the holiday issue of a magazine.

A group of women stood in the kitchen, where the island had been laid out with food, including pastries, muffins, fruit salad, two large breakfast frittatas, a platter of bacon and sausages, and homemade breads and jams.

Joy recognized Dana right away, and she came forward to give her a warm hug.

"As soon as we heard what happened, we wanted to do something," she said to Joy. "We're just so happy and relieved that Piper is okay."

"I can't believe it," Joy said, staring around her in awe. "What you've done is just—it's amazing."

"It was nothing, and we had a lot of fun doing it. C'mon, and I'll introduce you to the other ladies."

Joy didn't think she'd ever remember all of their names, but she was determined to try. Most of them were the wives or girlfriends of the firefighters, but there were two women who had just wanted to do something out of friendship with the Holliday family.

"This is Mia Davies, who runs the Snapdragon Inn B&B near the lake," Dana said. "I provide the muffins and pastries for the inn each morning. Her mother is Dot, who used to own the Ginger Snap."

"Dana's muffins are the main reason my guests keep coming back," Mia said with a wide smile. She extended her hand to Joy. "I'm so happy to meet you, and am so grateful that your little girl is okay."

Mia was lovely, with dark hair that fell straight and gleaming to skim her shoulders, and dark, expressive eyes that missed nothing.

"And this is Laurel Cavanaugh," Dana said, drawing another woman forward. "She's our local author."

Joy frowned. "Not the mystery novels?"

Laurel looked embarrassed, but she nodded. Her thick, auburn hair was pulled back in a ponytail, and she had a habit of adjusting her black-rimmed glasses, which were reminiscent of the ones worn by rocket scientists during the 1950s. "Yes, that's me."

The books that Cole had brought her to read at the hospital had been written by this woman. Joy had never met a real author before, and found she was a little tongue-tied.

"Wow, that's wonderful. I have two of your books, but I haven't read them yet." She didn't know if that sounded ungracious, so she hurried to explain. "I mean, I only got them last night, so I haven't had a chance to read them yet, but I will!"

Laurel laughed, and her smile transformed her otherwise plain features into something truly remarkable. "It's okay," she said reassuringly. "I'm not offended if you never read them. My own family hasn't read my books."

Before Joy could express her dismay at that little tidbit, Mia took her by the arm and drew her slightly away.

"I wanted to ask you…" she began cautiously. "Beth said you made these dishes." She indicated the stack of stoneware plates and mugs on the island.

Joy nodded. "Yes, that's right. I have a small potter's studio in Santa Barbara."

"Do you ship your stuff? Because it's absolutely gorgeous."

"I haven't, no. I sell it through several shops in California and Washington, but that's it."

"Would you consider shipping items to Montana, if I paid the cost?"

Joy couldn't contain her surprise. "Of course. What are you thinking of ordering?"

Mia smiled. "Oh, about fifty each of the plates, saucers, bowls and mugs. I'd also be open to purchasing accessory pieces, if you have them. I want to use your dishes exclusively at the Snapdragon Inn."

Joy stumbled back a step and reached out to steady herself.

"We'll talk later," Mia promised, grinning. "Right now, I think you're needed in the other room."

Joy heard Piper squealing in delight, and excused herself, still reeling from the news that someone wanted to purchase two hundred pieces of her pottery.

Two hundred pieces!

She'd received an insurance settlement after Matt's death, but had put it away for Piper's future. The money she made through her pottery sales had so far been enough to make ends meet, but this sale would enable her to do the small extras that had always been beyond her budget.

Making her way through the crowded kitchen, she found Piper sitting on the sofa in the great room, while Cole held the puppy for her. Montana squirmed against Cole's restraining hands, desperate to leap all over Piper. Eldon leaned on the back of the sofa and watched, chuckling softly at the puppy's antics.

"I can't just let him go, pipsqueak," Cole was saying. "He could hurt you without meaning to. Maybe in a couple of days, when your arm doesn't ache anymore."

Seeing Joy, he handed the puppy to Eldon, and made room for her on the sofa. "You holding up okay? You look as if you're about to collapse."

Joy kept her voice low. "I can't believe you did all of this, Cole. It's more than I could have ever imagined."

"We all wanted to do something," he replied. "After what happened—" He broke off. "We wanted to make sure Piper got her magical Christmas."

"But the way the whole fire station turned out to help..." She gestured helplessly. "I'm overwhelmed."

Cole gave a huff of laughter. "I never thought I'd hear myself say this, but I'm actually looking forward to Christmas."

Joy searched his eyes, and what she saw there was enough to stop her breath, just for an instant. Had she really believed she could keep this man from stealing her heart? After what he'd done for her and Piper, she was ready to hand it to him on a platter.

"Yes, I think it's going to be a pretty special day," she agreed.

The morning passed in a blur, as everyone convened in the kitchen to eat the delicious food that had been prepared.

When Piper showed signs of growing tired, and Joy announced she was going to tuck her in for a nap, people began saying their goodbyes and leaving, until finally it was just family.

"I don't want to go upstairs," Piper protested on a huge yawn.

"I don't think anyone is ready for you to leave their sight," Joy agreed. "You can take a nap down here, on the sofa."

Beth made Piper comfortable on the sofa with a pillow and a blanket, and even Montana had worn himself out enough that he was allowed to curl up next to her.

After Piper had fallen asleep, Beth brought out a tray of coffee and set it down on the table in front of the fire.

"Well," she said, sitting down on the sofa by Piper's feet, "I don't know about the rest of you, but I feel wrung out, both physically and emotionally. It's been quite a day."

Joy nodded her agreement. She sat in one of the leather chairs, and Cole sat in the chair next to her with his long legs stretched out.

Joy cradled her coffee in her hands and watched as Eldon threw another log onto the fire. "Thank you all so much for what you did. I think this is definitely a Christmas that Piper will remember for the rest of her life."

"It's going to be a memorable Christmas for all of us," Beth agreed.

Joy looked at Cole. "Somehow, I think you were the mastermind behind all of this."

"Nah. When I came home, Beth and Eldon were already

dragging the decorations out of storage. All I did was call in reinforcements, and oversee the selection of the biggest tree we could find."

"The truth is, we could have had a tragedy on our hands," Eldon said gruffly, walking over to the sofa to lay a hand on Piper's head. "Instead, Beth and I feel as if we've been given a second chance."

"We've been so steeped in our own grief since losing Matt, that we lost sight of our precious granddaughter," Beth added, and reached for a tissue. "She's his legacy, and we almost lost her." She wiped at her eyes. "So we wanted to create a fairytale Christmas for her."

Joy smiled gratefully. "I think you've done that."

"The only thing left to do," Eldon said, "is for her to put the star on the top of the tree. That used to be the boys' job, but I think we can transfer it to Piper."

"What's in that box, there?" Joy asked, indicating a cardboard box that had been pushed out of the way.

"Oh, I thought it might be nice for Piper to see pictures of her father when he was a little boy," Beth said. "I asked Eldon to pull the box out of the closet. There are pictures of Cole, too." She gave Cole a fond smile. "He was always so handsome, even as a child."

Joy could well believe that was true, and she laughed when Cole actually looked embarrassed by Beth's compliment.

"I would love to see the pictures, if you don't mind," Joy said.

Eldon pulled the box close to the sofa, and Joy moved to

sit next to Beth, so she could see the photo albums more clearly. Even Cole came to lean his forearms on the back of the sofa, his head close to Joy's as he looked over their shoulders. Only Eldon stayed near the fireplace and showed little interest in seeing the pictures. Instead, he frowned into the fire, and Joy suspected seeing photos of Matt was still too painful for him.

"Oh, my goodness," Beth exclaimed softly. "I had no idea this was in here."

Her face had gone soft, and Joy peered over her arm to see a framed photo of two teenaged girls, their arms flung around each other as they laughed into the camera. Beth was easily identifiable with her bright red hair and her freckles, but Joy didn't recognize the other girl.

"Who is that with you?" she asked.

"That was my best friend, Laney. She lived in town, and she was like a sister to me, from the time we were in kinder-garten. We were inseparable."

Joy studied the photo of the pretty blonde girl. "What happened to her? Does she still live in the area?"

"No, she moved away when we were in high school. We wrote letters for a while, and then we lost touch. I think about her sometimes."

"You could probably find her easily enough," Cole sug-gested. "With all the social media and accessibility to public records online, it probably wouldn't be that difficult."

Joy recalled Cole telling her his own search for his miss-ing father had turned up nothing. How long had it been since he'd done an online search?

Beth smiled up at Cole. "I may just do that. Laney Dupree was her name. I remember her father was a hard man. We were both terrified of him, and I only ever called him *sir*."

They laughed, and Beth put the photo away. Reaching into the box, she withdrew an album and opened it. "This is the one I wanted Piper to see. Matt and Cole must have been about ten or eleven, and they were hellions."

Joy looked at the photos, and her heart caught at the sight of Matt as a little boy. With his unruly red hair and freckles, he could easily have been mistaken for Piper. They looked so alike! Beside him, taller and skinnier, stood Cole. Even as boy, he'd had the same sharply angled features and serious gaze. Where Matt was laughing, Cole stared solemnly at the camera.

"Cole," she teased, "you haven't changed a bit, except that your hair was blonde!"

"Yes, I was blonde until I was teenager, and then my hair started to darken up."

They looked at photos until it began to grow dark outside, and Piper and Montana started to stir. Eldon sat in a leather club chair near the fire, dozing, and Cole had left about an hour earlier to take care of Lucy and the puppies.

"Time to put these away," Beth said, returning the albums to the box. "Looks like someone is waking up."

"I'll take Montana outside if you don't mind bringing Piper to the bathroom," Joy said. She picked up the warm, sleepy puppy and cuddled him in her arms as he yawned and then tried to lick her hands.

She snapped his leash on, unwilling to risk him wandering away, and then pulled her coat on and stepped outside. The night was dark and so cold, the snow squeaked beneath her feet, and her breath froze on the air. While Montana obediently did his duty, Joy tipped her head back and looked upward, entranced by how clear the night sky was. She'd never seen so many stars.

Headlights cut through the darkness, and she recognized Cole's pickup truck. She waited as he climbed out and crossed the yard to her side.

"Taking care of business, I see," he said, grinning as Montana greeted him.

"I can't believe how beautiful it is out tonight," she said. "We never see stars like this in Santa Barbara."

Cole looked up. "Yeah, it never gets old. There's not as much ambient light or smog out here, so you get a better view."

"It's absolutely beautiful."

"It sure is."

Something in his voice made Joy look at him, and she realized he no longer looked at the stars. He was looking at her. Even in the indistinct light, she recognized the expression in his eyes and a thrill of anticipation chased itself along her spine.

"Cole…"

"Are you doing okay?" he asked softly.

"I am now."

She smiled at him to let him know he hadn't misunderstood her. She didn't know what might happen between them, or if they even had a future together. But she knew a good man when she saw him, and Cole was one of the best.

"Joy," he said, and his voice sounded thick. "Come here."

He reached for her, and then she was in his arms. He slid his hands beneath her hair and tipped her face up, studying her in the darkness.

"Do you have any idea what you do to me?" he asked, and then he bent his head and kissed her. Despite the cold, his lips were warm as they explored hers, teasing her lips apart to taste her. Joy made a small sound of pleasure, and Cole shifted closer, until she was left in no doubt about how much he wanted her. Desire swirled through her. How long had it been since she'd felt this way? She'd almost forgotten the sweet, sharp tug of yearning.

"I want you," Cole said softly, and dragged his mouth along her jaw, until he reached the side of her neck, where his beard growth caused her to shiver. He took her earlobe between his teeth and bit down gently. "I can't think of anything except you."

"Cole..." She speared her fingers through his hair and brought his mouth back around to hers, kissing him with all the pent-up emotion and passion of the past few days. He groaned loudly and, reaching down, cupped her bottom and lifted her against him. She could feel how hard he was, and it only served to increase her own building need.

The bulb on the nearby lamp post suddenly snapped on, flooding the area with light and they broke apart. Joy realized she'd dropped Montana's leash when Cole had started kissing her, and now the puppy stood watching them, his ears cocked. Bending down, she retrieved the end of the lead. The door opened and Beth stuck her head outside.

"Joy, what are—oh!" She saw Cole and she smiled. "Cole! I had no idea you'd returned. Well, come in before you both catch cold!"

Without looking at each other, they filed into the house, but Joy was acutely conscious of Cole behind her, and wondered just how much Beth had seen.

"I'm glad you're here, Cole," she said as they followed her into the great room. "Piper wants to put the star on the tree, but she needs a little boost."

Piper gave a happy cry when she saw Cole and launched herself into his arms.

"Hey there, pipsqueak," he said, lifting her up. "How's the arm feeling?"

"Good! Mr. Tanner, can you lift me to the top of the tree?"

She held up a large, silver star. "I need to put this on the very top."

"I think that can be arranged," he told her.

Eldon was awake and, together, they walked over to the tree, which was still dark. As Piper clutched the star in her good hand, Cole lifted her over his head, holding her around the waist.

"Can you reach?" he asked.

"I think so!" Piper stretched forward and pushed the star down on the very top branch, which stuck straight up. "There! I did it!"

Beth, Eldon, and Joy clapped as Cole lowered Piper to the ground. The star leaned to one side, but they each declared it looked absolutely perfect.

"And now..." Eldon said dramatically, and flipped a switch on the wall, illuminating the tree with hundreds of colored lights so that even Joy gasped in delight.

"It's beautiful!" Piper shouted, jumping up and down as Montana barked in excitement.

Joy had to agree. It was the prettiest tree she had ever seen. The lights reflected in the large windows, making the effect even more dramatic, and she turned to Cole with a smile.

"It's the most perfect tree I've ever seen."

They stood admiring the tree for several moments, when Piper suddenly turned toward Joy.

"Mommy, we almost forgot your special ornament!"

For a moment, Joy stared blankly at her daughter, before she recalled the small box that she had carried with her from California. Immediately, guilt swept over her like an avalanche as she realized Piper was correct—she *had* forgotten the special ornament that Matt had given her on their last Christmas together.

Now she watched as Piper hurried up the stairs and reappeared a moment later, carrying the small wooden box in her good hand. Joy was aware of the curiosity of the others, as Piper carefully carried the box over to Joy. But as Piper handed the box to her, it slipped from her little fingers. Joy tried to catch it, sweeping her hand under the box as it fell, but she only succeeded in knocking it even further away. The box flew across the room and hit the hearth, where it broke open and spilled its precious contents against the stone.

Joy watched in horror as the fragile crystal ornament—a delicate hummingbird in flight—shattered, the shards glittering against the firelight. Piper gasped, looked at Joy with wide, stricken eyes, and promptly burst into tears.

For a moment, Joy thought she might cry, too. She swiftly recovered and caught Piper in a tight embrace, soothing the little girl.

"Shh," she said against Piper's hair. "Don't cry, it's okay. It was an accident, sweetheart."

But Piper only cried harder.

Over her daughter's head, she watched as Cole bent down and picked up the broken pieces, and put them back in the box. She recalled when Matt had given her the beautiful crystal hummingbird. She'd loved it, of course, but it had taken on a special significance after he was gone, when she began to see hummingbirds everywhere. Joy felt her throat tighten, but determinedly pushed down her sorrow.

"Piper, listen to me," she said, setting the child slightly away from her so that she could look at her. "I don't want you to be sad about this. It was just an accident."

"But—but my daddy gave that to you," she said, hiccupping.

"He did," Joy agreed. "But it's just an ornament. He gave me something far more precious, and I still have that."

"What is it?" Piper asked, swiping her fist across her eyes.

Joy smiled tenderly at her, and smoothed a bright tendril of hair back from her face. "You."

Piper gave her a tremulous smile, and Joy hugged her again.

Beth came forward and bent to kiss Piper's cheek, before taking her hand. "Why don't you come into the kitchen with Grammy and Grampy? I think maybe a glass of milk and a cookie are just the thing."

Joy watched as Piper went with Beth and Eldon into the kitchen, and then turned to see Cole use a dustpan and hand broom to sweep up the last slivers of crystal from the stone hearth. He closed the box, and angled his head to look at Joy.

She drew in a deep breath, and forced herself to smile at him. Did he think she and Piper were silly for becoming emotional over an ornament? What she'd told Piper was no less than the truth. While the ornament was a tangible reminder of her late husband, it was just an ornament. An inanimate object. Piper was everything.

"I'm okay," she assured Cole.

He stood up and came over to sit beside her on the sofa, the small box in his hand. "You sure?"

"Yes."

"I'm sorry for your loss."

For a moment, Joy wasn't certain if Cole referred to the ornament, or to Matt. Maybe both.

She listened for Piper's voice in the kitchen, and only after she was assured that the child was out of earshot did she reply, keeping her voice low.

"For a long time after Matt died, my life was like that crystal ornament—broken. I kept trying to pick up the pieces and put them back together, even though the shards hurt when I touched them." She took the box from him. "I know this sounds silly, but I feel as if each sliver of glass represents a memory we created. I don't want to shut those memories away in a box, or throw them away, but I can't live in the past, either. I have to look to the future—for myself and for Piper."

She raised her eyes to his, seeing compassion and understanding in the blue depths.

"Hey," he said, his voice gruff. "Come here."

Before she realized his intent, he drew her into his arms and held her close, one hand rubbing over her back. It was an embrace meant to comfort and soothe, and Joy let her head drop to his broad shoulder. It couldn't hurt to let someone else be the strong one, even for a few minutes, and she'd been carrying such a heavy burden for so long. Cole felt so good—strong and warm and alive. Joy could have stayed in his arms indefinitely, especially with his big hand stroking her back, but she pulled away when she heard Piper and her in-laws returning.

"Thank you," she said softly, and tucked the box into the cushion beside her.

Piper climbed into her lap, and Joy settled her there, kissing the top of her head. "All better?"

"Mm-hmm." She held up a cookie. "I brought you one, too, because Grammy says they make everything better."

Joy accepted the cookie. "Thank you. Your Grammy is a smart lady."

Piper twisted to look at Cole. "Did you get a tree for

your house yet? Because if you didn't, I saw lots of pretty ones in the woods!"

There was a loud commotion as the adults simultaneously laughed, groaned, and threatened Piper with early bedtime for the rest of her life if she even considered going outside without one of them.

Chapter Twelve

DESPITE HER PROTESTS, Joy insisted Piper spend the following day quietly indoors, either playing with the castle set that Eldon had brought down from the attic, or maybe working on a puzzle or reading books together. Piper complained loudly, claiming her arm didn't hurt at all, and that Cole had promised they would get a tree. But Joy was adamant, and Piper finally gave up, dragging her feet as she walked with slow and dramatic deliberation into the family room, her little shoulders slumped. Even the yellow Disney princess gown she wore seemed to droop a little. Only Montana seemed happy as he bounced beside her.

"I need her to be inside today," Joy said to Beth as they watched the little girl trail her blanket on the floor. "Maybe she is feeling better, but I think she should take it easy for a day or two."

"You don't need to explain anything to me," Beth said, as she gathered the ingredients for a homemade chicken stew with dumplings. "I completely understand. One down day won't hurt her, and she's more tired than she realizes." She gave Joy a reassuring smile. "Tomorrow is soon enough to get a tree for Cole. The boy has gone this long without having one; another day isn't going to matter."

Joy pulled a stool up to the island where Beth was work-ing. "Is he really that anti-Christmas?"

"Wouldn't you be, if your father left you in a rundown motel room on Christmas Eve?"

She had a point. But Cole didn't seem to mind if other people celebrated Christmas, and he'd even said he was glad that Piper still believed in Santa. Had he believed in Santa until that Christmas morning when he'd woken up alone, with no father and no Christmas gifts? Her heart ached for the innocent little boy he had been.

"What was he like, back then?"

Beth glanced up at Joy. "Matt and Cole were inseparable from the time Harley Ray Tanner showed up at the sawmill one summer morning, looking for work and dragging that poor boy along with him." She gave a soft laugh, lost for a moment in memory. "Although, to be fair, Cole didn't seem to mind. He was a bright, happy little boy, and he and Matt took to each other almost immediately."

Joy rested her chin on her palm. "What do you think happened to his father? Why do you think he left Cole behind?"

Just for an instant, anger clouded Beth's eyes and she stirred the dumpling batter with more force than necessary. "I always thought he was a drunk, but Eldon swears the man never touched a bottle. But he always—and I mean *always*—carried a large water bottle around with him, and I often thought it had more than water in it. Sometimes, when he walked, he'd weave and sway, and there were more than a few occasions when he seemed very confused about things." She sighed. "And he was terribly thin. He looked unhealthy."

"Could he have been sick?"

Beth paused and looked at Joy. "He might have been, but we'll never know. Eldon called every hospital within a five hundred mile radius. He notified the police, and even hired a private investigator, but we never learned what happened to him. After a year, I made him stop looking. By then, Cole was part of our family and I no longer wanted to find Harley Ray. Call me selfish, but I didn't want to risk losing Cole."

"I don't think that's selfish," Joy murmured. "I think it's incredibly loving and generous, and he's lucky he had you."

But her mind couldn't stop thinking about the man who had left his little boy behind on Christmas Eve. Even if he and Cole had argued, what kind of parent abandoned an eight year old?

Her thoughts were interrupted when the door opened, bringing a gust of cold air as Cole came in. He dropped his hat on a hook, and nodded at Beth and Joy, sniffing appreciatively as he came into the kitchen.

"Mmm, smells good," he said, peering into the large covered pot.

"Chicken stew," Beth confirmed, smiling. "What are you up to?"

"Well, I thought I'd drop by to check on the patient, and to bring her these." He drew his hand from behind his back and held out several DVD movies, fanning them like a deck of cards.

"Christmas movies?" Beth asked, leaning forward to peer at the covers.

"Well, kids' movies that take place around Christmas," Cole said defensively. "I thought Piper might like to watch them, since something tells me we won't be getting a tree today."

"I hope you don't mind," Joy said apologetically. "She insists she feels fine, but I'd rather keep her indoors today."

Cole looked at her, and his gaze was warm. "I get it. Where is the little pipsqueak?"

"She's pouting—I mean playing—in the other room," Joy smiled. "She'll be happy to see you."

Beth looked up and smiled when they heard Piper's glad cry of welcome when she saw Cole. "That will keep her busy for a while."

Joy peeked into the other room and watched as Cole inserted a movie and turned it on for Piper. But he didn't stay to watch it with the little girl and instead made his way down to Eldon's office.

"Does Cole work with Eldon on house designs?" she asked, hoping she sounded casual.

She had a perverse need to learn everything she could about Cole, even though she would eventually return to California. When they had been at The Drop Zone pub, he'd started to tell her about working with Eldon, but then the waitress had come and the conversation had ended. She'd wanted to ask Cole more about his future plans with the timber frame homes, but there hadn't seemed to be a good time.

Beth looked at her, a knowing glint in her eyes. "His house is quite something, isn't it?"

"It really is. He said he helped to design it, so I just wondered…"

"Eldon is hoping Cole will take over the business for him when he's ready to retire," Beth confided. She lowered her voice. "And I think Cole is actually considering it."

"Really."

"After Matt—" Beth broke off, and then seemed to square her shoulders. "About four years ago, Cole made a decision to become a seasonal firefighter and only work during the summer, so that he could spend more time helping Eldon with the business."

"I thought he spent the off-season skiing."

Beth laughed. "He does, every chance he gets. But he's also a big part of the company. He's been helping with the timber frame business since he was a teenager. I don't know what Eldon would do without him."

Joy considered what Beth had said. Would Cole take over the timber frame business after Eldon retired? Joy could easily envision Cole taking over the family business. He obviously had a talent for house design, and he was smart and capable, and *he wouldn't be jumping wildfires*. She wanted to ask more questions, but was afraid she'd already shown too much interest in Cole's personal life, and she wasn't ready to admit to anyone—even to herself—that she wanted him.

THERE WAS NO keeping Piper in the house the next day. She insisted they needed to get a tree for Cole, and she wouldn't be satisfied until they had found one for him, and had it in his house and decorated.

As promised, Cole came by after breakfast to pick them up.

"I think this may be a long day for you," Joy warned him, as she helped Piper into her coat and boots.

Today the little girl wore her bright pink tutu over a pair of jeans and a pink sweater, and the tulle puffed out from beneath the hem of her coat like a ruffle of pink frosting.

"Long days are the best kind," he replied, and gave Piper a conspiratorial wink. "Especially when you're in good company."

They said goodbye to Eldon and Beth, and made their way to Cole's pickup truck. He lifted Piper into the cab, securing her into her car seat.

"Are we going to the festibul first?" Piper asked. "I hope they still have some trees left!"

"Actually," he said, "I thought we could do some other fun stuff first."

"Like what?"

"Well... I was thinking ice-skating, but that's definitely off the list since we don't need you breaking your other arm, right?"

Piper giggled. "Right."

"But hot chocolate and a slice of pie never hurt anyone," he said, turning to help Joy up.

"Says you," she replied drily. "Have you ever heard the

154

saying, *once past the lips, forever on the hips?*"

Cole leaned in to secure her seatbelt, and as he pulled back, he looked directly into her eyes. "Trust me, darlin'," he said softly, "there's absolutely nothing wrong with your hips."

While she sat there and blushed, he closed the door and rounded the hood of the truck to climb behind the wheel.

"I thought we could start out at the diner, since we're going to need energy to sustain us through this long day," he said, putting the truck into gear. "Then we can try our hands—er, *hand*—at cow milking."

"Yes!" Piper fist-pumped the air with her good hand. "I've always wanted to milk a cow!"

Joy laughed. "You know it's just a pretend cow, right?"

"That's okay. I might be too scared to milk a *real* cow." She looked at Cole. "What will we do after we milk the pretend cow?"

"Hmm." He stroked his chin as he pretended to consider. "We could head over to Andersen's ranch, where they're doing horse-drawn sleigh rides, or decorate a gingerbread house at the Snapdragon Inn." He looked at Joy. "Mia Davies, who runs the inn, collaborated with Dana and built about three dozen gingerbread houses. They're selling tickets to decorate them today over at the inn. The proceeds go back into the recreation fund for next year's festival."

Piper sucked in her breath, and a smile wreathed her freckled face. "Maybe we can do both?"

"I think we could do both," Joy agreed, laughing. "As long as Cole doesn't mind."

"I can't think of anything I'd rather do," he said, and he even managed to sound sincere.

True to his word, they started at the diner, where they each had a slice of homemade apple pie, accompanied by hot chocolate for Piper, and coffee for Cole and Joy.

"Is this place always this busy?" Joy asked, as she watched the friendly interchange between the waitresses and the customers.

"Red's has been an institution in this town for as long as I can remember," Cole said. "Judging by the decor, I'd say this place has been open since the fifties. Maybe even before that."

The diner had a definite fifties vibe, with the original Formica tabletops, black and white tile floors, and red vinyl and stainless steel stools at the counter.

"I think it's charming," she said. "It must be nice living in a small town, where everyone knows everybody else."

"Where everyone knows everybody else's business, you mean," Cole said drily.

"Well, if you really minded, you wouldn't still be living here," Joy countered.

"You're right." He looked around the diner, and then out the window at the street, where people were enjoying the festival. "I can't really envision living anywhere else. I guess that's why I have such a hard time understanding—"

He broke off abruptly.

"Understanding what?" Joy asked.

"Nothing. It's nothing, really."

But as they left the diner, Joy couldn't help thinking that

he'd been about to say something important.

Something revealing.

Something about Matt, maybe.

Had he been upset when Matt had left Glacier Creek to resettle in California? Joy had offered to move out to Montana, but Matt wouldn't hear of it. Her pottery business had just been getting started, and her family lived nearby. He'd insisted on moving out to California, saying he could fight fires anywhere, but her chances of establishing herself as an artist were better on the west coast than they were in Glacier Creek. In the end, she hadn't argued, but she could see his decision to leave Montana must have been a difficult one—with every day that passed, Joy found herself more charmed by the area and the people who lived here.

After they finished eating, they walked over to the common where several wooden cows, outfitted with rubber udders, had been set up. Cole and Joy stood in line with Piper, waiting for their turn to "milk" the cows. Cole declared they would make a contest out of it, with Joy and Piper comprising one team, while he made up the second team.

"Hmm," Joy mused, "that doesn't seem fair. We'll have three hands to your two."

"What does the winner get?" Piper asked, hanging on Cole's hand and giving him a winning smile.

Cole laughed, and swung the little girl up into his arms. "I suppose if it's a contest then there should be a prize," he conceded. Over the top of Joy's head, he winked at Joy. "What should the prize be?"

Piper put one finger on her chin, pretending to consider. "I know!" she said. "If me and Mommy win, then I get to stay up late tonight and you have to watch a movie with us."

"What if I win?"

Piper let her shoulders droop, and her voice turned despondent. "Then I'll go to bed on time."

"Without any complaining," Joy added, reaching out to tweak the end of one red curl.

In the end, Joy and Piper won, but only because Cole let them. Neither Piper nor Joy had been able to get any liquid to squirt out of the udders and into the plastic buckets, until one of the event coordinators had finally relented and showed them the trick to squeezing the rubber fingers. Even then, they'd barely managed to accumulate any liquid by the time the buzzer rang, but Cole had somehow managed to acquire even less liquid in his bucket.

He accepted the friendly jibes of the small crowd that had gathered to watch with laughter and good humor, before declaring Piper the victor.

"Yes!" she cried with satisfaction. "And I get to pick the movie!"

Following his defeat, Cole drove them out to the outskirts of Glacier Creek, where the land opened up to wide, snow-covered plains, and cattle stood side by side against the bitter wind, their breath steaming on the frosty air. Piper, who had never seen real cows before, stared with undisguised interest at the herds.

"Why don't they go inside a barn?" she asked.

"There are too many of them, for one thing," Cole explained. "And they're pretty well equipped to stay outside, even when it's cold." He looked at the little girl. "Don't you worry about them."

"What do they eat when the fields are buried in snow?" Joy asked. She had little knowledge of ranching or cattle, and found this aspect of rural life interesting.

"The rancher will provide them with all the hay they can eat, and they'll also receive protein supplements and salt licks. For a healthy cow, that's usually sufficient to see them through the winter. A good windbreak also helps them through any severe weather."

They turned through a gate and onto a road that was lined with trucks and cars, and, up ahead, Joy saw an enormous barn and numerous outbuildings. The barn doors had been thrown open, and inside, Joy caught a glimpse of glittering mini-lights, and hay bale tables stacked with hot thermoses and baked goods. Standing beside the barn were two beautiful sleighs, each drawn by two draft horses. Piper sat up higher in her car seat, her eyes round as she looked at them.

"They're so pretty" she breathed.

Joy had to agree. One sleigh was red and had three bench seats behind the driver. The other was green, and was longer, with four bench seats. Each had been embellished with gold painted trim and decorative winter scenes, and bright gold bells dangled from the front.

As they exited the truck and walked toward the sleighs, one of the horses shook his head and whinnied, making the bells on his harness jingle merrily. Piper was entranced.

There was one bench on the smaller sleigh still available, so Cole quickly reserved the space for the three of them, lifting Piper into the middle, and helping Joy to climb in after her. Piper was momentarily distracted when the driver came around to the far side of the sleigh to chat with her.

"Hey," Cole said softly.

Joy turned toward him. He stood leaning with his forearms on the edge of the sleigh so that they were almost eye-level. Before she could guess his intent, he dipped his head and pressed a brief, warm kiss against her mouth. When he pulled away, he was smiling.

"Sorry," he said, sounding anything but apologetic. "I've been dying to do that all morning."

Joy glanced at Piper, but the little girl was listening to their driver as he told her the names of the horses, and not paying any attention to Joy and Cole.

"I hope you can do better than that," she teased quietly, but her heart had already begun to thump hard against her ribs. The expression in his eyes made her feel a little weak as he leaned forward again, and this time fused his mouth to hers in a kiss that was devastatingly thorough.

"Mommy!"

They broke guiltily apart, and Joy turned to Piper with a bright smile, expecting a million questions. "What, baby?"

"The horses' names are Whiskers and Freckles! Aren't those silly names?"

Joy agreed they were, grateful that Piper hadn't seen the intimate exchange. She and Cole exchanged a look of relief, before he rounded the sleigh and climbed in on the other side of Piper. The driver provided them with a heavy, red wool blanket to put across their laps, and a thermos of hot chocolate with three metal cups, and then the driver took his place at the front of the sleigh, and they were off.

Sitting at the back of the sleigh, as they traversed the snow-packed road that wound along the fields, Joy felt as if she had stepped back in time. Once they reached the forest, they glided along trails between evergreens heavy with snow. The only sound was the swish of the metal runners, the crunching of snow beneath the horses' hooves, and the rhythmic jingling of the harnesses. This was Christmas as Joy had always envisioned it, through a prism of nostalgic greeting cards and Norman Rockwell paintings.

She turned to look at Piper. The little girl's cheeks and nose were pink with cold, but her blue eyes were bright with pleasure. When she slid her glance past Piper, to Cole, she realized he was watching her, and the expression in his eyes caused her to go warm beneath the heavy blanket. He looked rugged and handsome in his brimmed hat, with his collar turned up, and she noticed that Piper had snuggled up against his side as if it was the most natural thing in the world.

Joy's heart constricted. She wanted this man, even more than she dared to admit. He was still a seasonal firefighter, but if Beth was right, there was a possibility he could give that up. Fighting wildfires had been a huge part of Matt's life. It had been in his blood and nothing Joy had said could convince him to quit. Joy had no right to ask Cole to leave the forest service, but she clung to the hope he might actually accept Eldon's offer to take over the family business. If he didn't, she couldn't see a future with him.

Cole held up the thermos in one gloved hand, and raised an eyebrow in question. She nodded, and watched as he carefully poured them each a mug of steaming chocolate. He handed one to Joy, and then helped Piper to drink hers, holding the mug for her so she could keep her arms beneath the blanket. He seemed completely at ease helping the little girl, and laughed when she smacked her lips and grinned at him, displaying her chocolate moustache.

Joy looked quickly away. She didn't want to fall in love with Cole Tanner; didn't want her little girl to fall in love with him, either. She'd never felt so conflicted in her life. She couldn't forget the potency of his kisses, and there was a part of her that ached to feel his touch against her bare skin. She hadn't been intimate with anyone in nearly four years, and the thought of sharing that kind of intimacy with Cole caused a shiver of awareness to run through her.

Cole's shrewd gaze missed nothing. "Are you cold?"

"No."

He gave her a speculative look and, for a moment, Joy was certain he knew the direction of her thoughts. Flustered, she bent her head and sipped her hot chocolate, acutely conscious of his eyes on her.

When the sleigh ride came to an end, they spent several moments inside the barn, looking at the crafts and baked goods for sale, before Piper complained that she was cold.

"Why don't we go into town and grab lunch, before we head over to the Snapdragon Inn to decorate a gingerbread house," Cole suggested. "We can pick up a tree afterwards, and bring it back to my place."

"Are we going to help you decorate it?" Piper asked.

For just an instant, Cole looked alarmed, but he nodded brusquely. "Sure. Absolutely."

They stopped at a cozy little pizza restaurant, and Piper munched on a slice of cheese pizza while she chatted to the waitress who came over to admire her neon pink cast.

Joy leaned in toward Cole. "Why can't we help you decorate your tree?" she asked in a whisper.

He stared at her for a moment, and then bent his head to speak into her ear. "Because I don't own any decorations."

Now it was Joy's turn to stare. "Really?"

"Really."

"How is that even possible?"

"I've never had a tree at my house," he muttered. "When I did celebrate Christmas, it was always at Beth and Eldon's house, never mine."

Joy cast a quick glance across the table at Piper, but she was fully engrossed in telling the waitress about their sleigh ride.

"So you have no decorations?" She couldn't keep the shock out of her voice.

"Not a single bulb," he confirmed. "I already told you; I don't usually celebrate Christmas. I'm making an exception this year."

"Mommy, I'm all done!"

Joy swiveled around and smiled brightly at Piper. "Alright, then! Time to go decorate a gingerbread house!"

The Snapdragon Inn was situated on a knoll overlooking a private bay on Flathead Lake, with sweeping views down the lake to the distant mountains. Joy didn't know what she'd expected, but not the sprawling, turreted house with its shingled and stone exterior, surrounded by towering pines. The wide veranda that encircled the house had been trimmed in evergreen boughs and twinkle lights, and a large wreath adorned the entry door.

Inside, Joy heard a murmur of voices and laughter from deeper in the house, and Christmas music played softly, piped in through unseen speakers. Inside the hallway stood a Christmas tree, sparkling with lights and glass ornaments. From where they stood, Joy could see the entire interior of the house had been paneled in a rich, warm wood. The coffered ceilings were also wood, and a wide, mahogany staircase marched upward to a second floor landing beneath an enormous, arched window. Joy was still staring around her as she removed her coat, when Mia Davies appeared.

"Well, hello," she said, beaming at them. "Welcome to the Snapdragon Inn. I was hoping you'd come by. Here, let me take your coats."

Mia looked pretty in a deep red blouse with matching crystal earrings that set off her dark hair and eyes. Now she smiled at Piper.

"I have two open seats saved for you and your mom in the dining room." She held out her hand. "Do you want to come with me?"

Piper took Mia's hand, leaving Joy and Cole with no option but to follow them down the hallway. They passed two other rooms, and Joy peeked inside each. The first room was a large parlor with leaded windows that looked out to the covered veranda. There was a Christmas tree in this room, as well, decorated to match the color scheme of the room. A granite fireplace dominated the room, and there were numerous sofas and chairs arranged in cozy clusters. The sheer size of the room was astounding.

"Wow," Joy murmured to Cole. "This place is amazing."

"The house was originally built as a wedding gift for Margaret Davies and her husband, from her parents, at the turn of the century. It's been in the same family for more than a hundred years."

"They must have been very wealthy."

"Margaret was from Connecticut, and her father made his fortune on Wall Street and in lumber." He gave a sardonic smile. "I think they were comfortable."

The second room was a library, also richly paneled with yet another fireplace and several comfortable chairs for reading. An older couple sat near the fire, enjoying a hot drink and a plate of pastries from a nearby table.

"How many rooms does the house have?" Joy asked.

"There are twenty rooms," Mia said. "The house has twelve bedrooms, each with their own bathroom. There's also a tea house down by the lake with its own fireplace. That's always a favorite of the guests."

"And you're open year-round?"

"Oh, yes. Glacier Creek is becoming something of a tourist destination because of its proximity to the lake in the summer, and the ski resort in the winter."

"And you run it yourself with just your mother?"

Joy couldn't imagine the effort involved in maintaining such a huge house, never mind the surrounding property.

"I have some staff who help me," Mia said, laughing. "I could never do it on my own. My mom is a big help, now that she no longer owns the bakery, and I have two girls who come in from town each morning to help clean the rooms."

"How long has it been an inn?"

"The house went into foreclosure about fifteen years ago, and it sat empty for a long time," Mia said. "I lived on the East Coast back then, and didn't even know the place existed." Seeing Joy's expression of disbelief, she pulled a face. "It's a long story. Anyway, about five years ago, I scraped together enough money to make an offer, and the bank accepted it. I opened the inn a year later. Here we are."

They passed through the large, arched doorway of a third room, filled with people and the sounds of conversation and laughter. Joy saw they were in an enormous dining room, intricately paneled in a deep mahogany. The high ceilings were coffered in mahogany, as well, and a curving wall of windows looked out over a stone verandah and the lake. The room should have felt dark and oppressive, but a fire crackled in the granite fireplace at the far end of the room, and the wall of windows at the other end flooded the room with light. Both the mantle and windows had been decorated with cedar boughs and silver bells, and a Christmas tree graced one corner of the room.

Six small, round tables with chairs had been placed by the windows and around the perimeter of the room stood several buffet tables, displaying silver tea and coffee sets.

Dominating the center of the room was a long, rectangular dining table, covered now in a white plastic tablecloth.

Joy heard Piper's indrawn breath and understood. At least a dozen children crowded around the table, each with a gingerbread house in various stages of decoration. Running down the center of the table were bowls containing every kind of candy imaginable, and each child had a squeezable container of white frosting "glue."

"Here's your seat," Mia said, and led Piper to a chair near the center of the table. "There's a chair for your mom, too, so she can help you reach what you need."

Joy smiled at Mia. "Thank you so much. Did you make all these gingerbread houses?"

Mia pulled a face. "No, it was all Dana. I helped, but she did most of the work. We formed an assembly line of sorts, and we were able to whip them out pretty quickly. The fun part is the decorating."

She turned and indicated an elaborately decorated gingerbread house on one of the sideboards, larger than those that the children were working on, complete with spun glass windows and doors.

"That's incredible," Joy said, admiring the beautiful gingerbread house. "Really, it's a work of art. I just have a hard time believing you use this room for this purpose. Aren't you afraid the carpets will get ruined with the frosting, or something will get broken?"

Mia shrugged. "Not really. And what's the point of having something beautiful if you can't enjoy it? I've been holding this event every year since the inn opened, and the worst that's happened is one child got sick from eating too much candy."

They got Piper settled in her seat, and Mia brought her an unadorned gingerbread house, and showed her how to apply the frosting so that the candy would adhere.

Cole touched Joy's arm. "Listen, this could take a while. I have a few errands I need to run, so why I don't go take care of that, let Lucy and the pups out, and then I'll come back to collect you?"

"Are you sure?" Joy asked. "I can call Eldon to come and get us, if you'd rather."

She preferred that Cole come back for them, but he'd already sacrificed so much of his day for them, and she didn't want him to feel that he had to keep them entertained.

"I promised Piper we'd get a Christmas tree," he said, "and I keep my promises. I'll see you in a couple of hours."

Joy nodded. She had an almost irresistible urge to lean up and kiss him, and crossed her arms around her middle to keep from acting on the impulse. As if he understood, he nodded brusquely, said goodbye to Piper, and left. Despite the other parents and children surrounding her, the room seemed bigger and emptier without him in it.

"C'mon, Mommy," Piper said, patting the empty chair next to hers. "Come help me. I can't reach the gumdrops without you!"

With a last look at where Cole had left, Joy sat down. While she looked forward to sharing this event with Piper, she missed Cole's presence and realized her enjoyment of Glacier Creek was beginning to depend more on him than anything else.

Chapter Thirteen

COLE WRAPPED UP his errands as quickly as he could, including the delivery of two pups to nearby families. When he returned less than two hours later, Piper had finished her gingerbread house, and Mia was carefully wrapping it in cellophane and tying it closed with ribbon. The little house was a colorful collision of candy and frosting, and Cole's back teeth ached just looking at it.

"Hey, pipsqueak, that's pretty nice," he said, admiring her handiwork. "Did you have fun?"

"Yes!" Piper declared. "Now let's go get your tree!"

Cole looked at Joy over the little girl's head, and gave her a rueful grin. "Does she ever wind down?"

Joy arched an eyebrow. "This is a kid on a sugar-high. I did warn you that it would be a long day. What time is it, anyway?"

"About four o'clock." He glanced toward the windows, where the sun had already dropped behind the distant mountains. "It'll be dark in another half hour or so."

"Okay, peanut," Joy said, helping Piper down from her chair. "Let's go get a tree. And no falling asleep in the car!"

"I won't fall asleep," Piper said with indignation.

"Of course you won't," Joy said, grinning at Cole. "All that sugar will keep you going for hours yet."

Joy said goodbye to Mia, promising to come back so they could further discuss the details of the pottery purchase. Cole drove them back into town, listening as Piper talked animatedly about the gingerbread house and the other children she had made friends with. He parked the truck and they walked through the festival to the spot where the Glacier Creek firefighters were still selling holiday trees and greenery. Darkness had fallen, but Main Street sparkled beneath the lights that had been strung across the length of the road. The Christmas tree lot was brightly lit, and Scott Ross looked relieved to see them.

"Finally, a customer! I think you might be the last person in Glacier Creek who hasn't bought a tree yet," he said, slapping Cole on the back. "We're breaking the lot down tomorrow and packing up."

"Okay, let's see what you have left," Cole said. He hoped he hadn't waited too long. He'd never brought a Christmas tree into his house before, but he didn't want his first tree to be a Charlie Brown tree.

As Scott had implied, the remaining trees had been pretty well picked over, and Cole thought they were a rather pathetic looking bunch. But then Joy and Piper called him to the back of the lot, where a small pile of trees still lay on the ground, half-buried under the snow and tied with twine.

"Let's see what we have here," he said, crouching down to cut the cord with a pocket knife. He lifted the first tree out and stood up, giving it a vigorous shake. Snow showered onto the ground, and the branches fell partially open. The tree stood nearly as tall as Cole. It looked skinny to him, but maybe it would fill out as the branches relaxed.

"What do you think?" he asked Piper.

She leaned against Joy and studied the tree with a critical eye. "It's perfect!" she finally declared.

Cole cocked his head and studied the tree again. "Really?"

"Yup!"

"Okay, then," he said. "That was easier than I anticipated."

Joy laughed. "I think she's anxious to get home and decorate it."

Cole kept his expression carefully neutral. Did she even realize that she had referred to his house as *home*? Unbidden, he had an image of the three of them living in his house. He pictured a cheerful, chaotic scene with Piper and two dogs, and saw Joy creating her pottery in a room on the lower level of the house. He saw one of his upstairs bedrooms transformed into a princess-themed room, and then he pictured Joy in his big bed, her lustrous hair spread out across his pillow, and her slender limbs wound around him.

He was jerked back to reality when Scott thumped him on the back. "Found one, huh?"

Cole looked at Joy, who was watching him with a curious expression. He had an instant of panic when he thought she must know what he'd been thinking. Then she smiled and bent down to talk in Piper's ear.

"Tell Mr. Tanner that he has to actually buy the tree and

put it in his truck," she said, smiling.

Cole was glad for his hat and upturned collar, so she couldn't see his ears turning red. He paid for the tree, and on impulse, purchased a wreath for his door and another one for over the fireplace mantle.

"And that's the extent of my Christmas spirit," he growled, but without any real malice.

But Piper and Joy just laughed as he loaded the greenery into the back of his truck. As they drove to his house, he tried to recall the Christmases of his youth, before his father had taken off. Had they ever celebrated Christmas together? He had a fuzzy memory of one Christmas morning spent on a beach, when his father had given him a boogie board, and he'd ridden the surf all day while his dad had sat in the sand with a cooler, and watched. He couldn't have been more than five or six, and he had no idea what beach they'd been at, or even what part of the country they'd been in. But he knew he'd enjoyed that day.

Cole couldn't think of his childhood without feeling bitter. His father hadn't even left him with a sense of identity. Without a birth certificate, he had no idea who his mother was, or where he'd come from. He knew almost nothing about his father, or his early life. If it hadn't been for Eldon, he might have gone into foster care and become a statistic. Instead, Eldon had given him a home, had raised him alongside Matt, had petitioned the courts to provide him with a social security number. He'd encouraged him to follow his dream of becoming a firefighter, although Cole often wondered if that hadn't been Matt's dream, and he had just gone along for the ride.

Fighting wildfires side by side with Matt had been exhilarating. Nothing could defeat them, not when they dropped in from the skies, and then battled the blaze from the ground. They'd been young and invincible, and Cole had felt like a freaking superhero. That all changed when Matt transferred to the California hot shot crew, leaving smoke-jumping—and Cole—behind.

At first, Cole hadn't believed Matt would stay on the West Coast. But as the months passed, he realized Matt wasn't coming back to Montana. That was when battling wildfires had lost some of its glamor. And when Matt had been killed, Cole almost quit fighting fires altogether. As it was, he'd cut back to seasonal, and had turned his off-season attention to skiing and helping Eldon with the timber frame business.

At his house, Cole carried the tree inside, while Piper and Joy each carried a wreath. He'd left both the outside and interior lights on, remembering that Piper had been scared when she'd first seen her grandparent's dark house.

"Here we go," he said, carrying the tree into the kitchen, and leaning it against a timbered pole. "Wait here for just a sec."

He walked through the family room to where the puppies were kept, and came back carrying Montana.

"My puppy!" Piper exclaimed in surprise, as Cole carefully placed the squirming dog in her arms. Piper kissed the puppy's face. "How did he get here?"

"I had to stop by Beth and Eldon's place," Cole explained to Joy, "and I figured Piper would be happier if Montana was here with her."

"I'm sure Eldon appreciated that," Joy said. "He probably wasn't overly thrilled about taking care of a puppy all day."

"Nah," Cole said, hanging his hat on a hook and removing his coat. "Lucy comes from a long line of Holliday dogs, and Eldon has always had at least one—usually two—dogs on the property."

Joy removed her coat, and then bent to help Piper take her coat and boots off. "Why doesn't he have one now?"

"His last dog passed about three years ago, and he never replaced her."

Lucy padded into the kitchen to greet them, tail wagging, and one puppy bounded beside her.

"Who's this?" Joy asked, scooping the small dog up and cuddling it. "And where are the others?"

"This is the last one left," Cole said, coming over to rub behind the puppy's ears. "She's Number Three. The others have all gone to their new homes. I was actually considering giving this one to Eldon. As much as he grumbles about not wanting another dog, I think he'd enjoy having one around."

"You're going to give Montana's sister to Grampy?" Piper asked, looking up from where she was playing on the floor with Montana.

"Do you think that's a good idea?" Cole asked, as if his decision depended wholly on her response.

"Well…" Piper considered. "Grampy likes Montana, and I think they have fun together… so, yes!"

Cole gave an affirmative nod. "Good. We'll put a pretty red bow around her neck, and give her to him on Christmas morning."

"Yay!" Piper sat down on the floor with Montana still in her arms, while the second puppy climbed over her legs, whining with eagerness, and making the little girl laugh.

As he carried the tree into the family room, Joy stared at the tree stand and three plastic bins of lights and ornaments on the floor near the windows.

"What's this?" she asked.

Cole had the grace to look chagrined. "Beth gave them to me," he admitted. "Otherwise, we'd have had nothing to decorate with."

Cole started a fire in the massive fireplace, and then turned on some Christmas music. While he strung lights on the tree, Joy and Piper rummaged through his kitchen and put together a platter of sandwiches. Joy carried the food into the family room and set it down on a side table, out of reach of the curious puppies.

"That looks beautiful!" Joy declared when Cole finished, and turned the lights on. "This room needed a Christmas tree."

Cole turned to see she had curled up on his sofa with a mug of hot tea cradled in her hands, her stockinged feet tucked beneath her. Piper twirled in circles in front of the fire, admiring her pink tulle skirt as it swirled out around her legs. She munched on half of a sandwich and laughed as the puppies jumped against her legs and tried to steal the food from her hand.

Cole couldn't remember a time when his house had seemed so warm and inviting.

So complete.

For the first time since he'd built the house and moved in, it felt like a real home. And it had everything to do with Joy and Piper, and even the dogs. Unfamiliar with the sudden wave of emotion, he turned back to the tree and pretended to fiddle with the electrical cord. He couldn't believe that when Joy had arrived, he'd been prepared to resent her. Now he didn't know if he could let her go.

They spent the next several hours alternately eating, and hanging ornaments on the tree, until Piper declared she was done.

"It's almost seven," Joy said, as she and Cole hung the last of the ornaments, and closed up the empty bins. "Maybe we should get going."

"No!" Piper sat up from where she'd been sprawled on the couch. "You promised I could stay up late and watch a movie!"

"She's right," Cole said. "We did agree that was the prize for being the best pretend-cow milker this side of the Continental Divide."

"Hmm." Joy looked at Piper. "I don't know... she looks pretty tired, and a movie would put her way past her bedtime."

"I'm not tired, Mommy! You *promised*."

"If it makes a difference, Beth did send this over," Cole said, and retrieved a small duffel bag from where he'd stashed it earlier, near the kitchen door.

He watched as Joy unzipped it, and warm color swept into her face. She looked up at Cole. "Beth sent this over?"

"Yep. She said you'd want those."

Digging into the duffel bag, Joy pulled out a pair of Piper's pajamas, and then her own flannel lounge pants and an oversized Henley.

She raised her eyes to his. "She also packed clean underclothes, a hairbrush, and both of our toothbrushes." Her eyes narrowed. "Just what, exactly, did you tell Beth?"

Cole shrugged. "Just that we planned to watch a movie with Piper. She said you might want to stay over if Piper fell asleep."

Piper looked indignant. "I am *not* going to fall asleep!"

Joy was clearly unconvinced, but she took Piper upstairs, and when they returned, they both wore their pajamas. Cole couldn't contain his satisfaction.

"We're more comfortable in these," Joy said defensively.

Cole spread his hands wide and grinned. "I'm not judging. I want you to be comfortable."

Piper selected a movie, and Cole turned off the lights, so that the room was illuminated only by the flickering firelight, and the Christmas tree. He brought out a pillow and a soft throw for Piper, and despite the little girl's adamant declarations that she would not fall asleep, she obediently curled up at one end of the sofa with Montana tucked against her.

JOY SETTLED ON the opposite end of the sofa next to Cole, with Piper's small feet pressed against her hip, and gratefully accepted a glass of wine, while he enjoyed a bottled beer. The Christmas movie Piper had selected was lighthearted and funny, and Joy found herself watching Cole as he laughed out loud with Piper during the silly parts. His laugh was deep and infectious, and Joy found herself smiling at the sound.

By the time the movie was over, Piper was sound asleep and Joy was feeling comfortably buzzed from the two glasses of wine she'd consumed. Her gut told her she should pack Piper up and return to her in-law's house, but she was warm and cozy, and reluctant to leave the comfort of Cole's house.

Reluctant to leave Cole.

"I should probably go," she finally murmured, but knew her words lacked conviction.

"Stay here tonight," Cole said quietly, shifting sideways on the sofa to look at her. "I have three bedrooms upstairs. There's no need to take Piper out into the cold, not when she's already asleep."

"Cole..." She was so tempted.

"Let me carry her upstairs."

Joy looked at her daughter. The little girl was curled on her side with her good hand tucked beneath her chin, her mouth parted in sleep. Montana lay stretched out beside her, and one of his back legs kicked reflexively in sleep. Did she really want to wake them up and carry them out into the cold?

"What will Beth and Eldon think if we spend the night

here?" she protested. "I don't want them to get the wrong idea."

"What idea is that?"

She flushed. "That you and I—"

Cole shifted, and tipped his head down to look into her eyes. "I think it's too late for that, since Beth is the one who suggested you stay over, and packed your bag."

Joy flushed. Had she been that obvious? Even if Beth suspected that Joy might have feelings for Cole, she had a difficult time believing Beth would condone her staying at Cole's house. She'd been married to Beth's son, and Cole had been his best friend. Unless Beth truly had no inkling of Joy's growing feelings toward Cole.

Joy looked at Piper again. The child murmured something in her sleep and shifted, a quick frown furrowing her smooth brow. She turned to Cole.

"I'm not sure…"

He must have sensed her wavering, because he leaned toward her and covered her mouth with his. He tasted like the rich porter he'd had earlier and something else— something more intoxicating. Joy found herself moving closer and deepening the kiss. His tongue mated with hers, and he slid one hand into her hair and angled her face for better access. The sensation of his tongue against hers caused a jolt of pure need to spiral through Joy. She wanted to climb onto his lap. She wanted to straddle his hard thighs and wrap her arms around his head while he kissed her like—

"Mommy?"

The sleepy voice had them springing apart. Joy turned to see Piper watching them with drowsy eyes. She was more asleep than awake, and Joy knew she would likely recall nothing the following morning.

"What is it, baby?" Her voice sounded high and breathless, even to her own ears.

"Do you love Mr. Tanner?"

The question took Joy by surprise, and her face went hot with guilt and embarrassment.

"C'mon, sweetie," she said, evading the question. She couldn't bring herself to look at Cole. "Why don't I carry you up to bed?"

She stood up, prepared to lift Piper in her arms, but Cole was there before her.

"I'll carry her upstairs." He picked up the sleeping puppy and placed it in Joy's arms. The puppy scarcely moved as she watched Cole carefully lift Piper in his arms. The little girl's eyes were already drifting closed again. Joy followed Cole upstairs and into the bedroom where she and Piper had changed into their pajamas earlier that night. Cole laid the child in the center of the big bed, and Joy placed Montana on the blanket beside her, and then gently tucked Piper in, kissing her forehead.

"It's only nine-thirty," Cole said quietly. "I'm not planning to turn in for a while yet. Would you like to watch another movie?"

In the dim light from the hallway, Joy could barely see Cole's face, and couldn't make out his expression. But she knew if she returned downstairs with him, she wouldn't resist him if he indicated he might be interested in anything beyond watching television. The thought was both thrilling and terrifying, and suddenly she was too much of a coward to actually act on her desires.

"I'll stay with Piper," she whispered.

In the dim light that filtered into the bedroom from the hallway, she saw Cole nod, but she couldn't make out his expression.

"Okay," he said. "Sleep well. There's a nightlight on the side table if you need it. There are clean towels in the bathroom. If you're up before me, help yourself to anything in the kitchen."

"I will, thanks."

"Goodnight."

She listened to as his footsteps receded down the stairs, and then slowly sat down on the edge of the mattress, reaching over to switch on the nightlight. The only sound in the bedroom was Piper's soft breathing. Joy rubbed her palms over the tops of her thighs and blew out a hard breath. It was barely nine-thirty, and she was far from tired.

Just the opposite.

She was a bundle of nerves, and sitting in the dark room, she was certain she'd made a huge mistake in telling Cole she'd rather stay upstairs with Piper. If she was honest with herself, she'd rather be downstairs, with him.

Whatever that entailed.

But she hadn't been with anyone in such a long time, and being with Cole would be intense and amazing, and would make her feel so… vulnerable.

Turning, she looked at her sleeping daughter, and softly stroked her hair. Piper opened her eyes.

"I didn't mean to wake you up," Joy whispered. "Go back to sleep; everything is fine."

Piper yawned and turned on her side. "Mommy," she said, her voice slurred with sleep. "I saw you kiss Mr. Tanner. Do you love him?"

Joy bent over and kissed her daughter's soft cheek. "I don't know, baby. Maybe I do."

She expected Piper to respond, but the little girl had already fallen back asleep. She waited until Piper's breathing grew even and regular. Then she drew in a deep, calming breath and stood up, and made her way downstairs.

Cole was in the kitchen, cleaning up the dishes from their evening. Joy stood quietly and watched him for several minutes, admiring the ease and efficiency of his movements. He'd removed his heavy chamois shirt and wore only a faded red tee shirt. With each movement, his muscles bunched and flexed beneath the thin fabric, and the sight of his thick biceps made her mouth go dry. As if sensing her presence, he paused, and then turned around. He stilled when he saw her, and Joy thought she saw both wariness and hope in his blue eyes.

"I couldn't sleep," she said, and walked toward him.

"Not tired?" he asked.

"Not in the slightest," she admitted, and reached for him. "I can think of others things I'd rather do than sleep."

As his arms came around her and their lips met, Joy felt as if she'd finally found her way home.

Chapter Fourteen

COLE WOKE UP alone in his big bed the following morning, but he'd expected that. What he hadn't expected was how mind-blowing the previous night had been. The sex had been hot and urgent and deeply satisfying.

That had been the first time. And then it had been hot and unhurried, and even more gratifying.

His body still hummed with pleasure. Joy had risen before dawn, and after one long, intense kiss, had retreated upstairs before Piper woke up. Cole had never invited a woman to stay at his place before, and he'd always thought if that should happen, he'd want her gone before sunrise. But, with Joy, the opposite was true.

He wanted her to stay.

He wanted her, pure and simple. Any way he could get her.

Upstairs, he heard the shower running, and he closed his eyes and pictured Joy standing under the stream of water. Her scent still clung to his pillow and bedclothes, and he found himself getting turned on all over again. With a groan, he flung back the covers and stood up. If anyone needed a shower, it was him.

A cold one.

Twenty minutes later, Piper and Joy joined him in the kitchen, with Montana squirming in Joy's arms.

He devoured the sight of her, and she responded with a self-conscious smile. "Good morning."

"Good morning. Hey, Pipsqueak."

"I'm just going to take him outside," Joy said, indicating the puppy. "He was good enough to hold it all night."

Cole arched an eyebrow. "At least we hope he did."

Joy gave a surprised laugh, and then stepped outside with Montana. Piper scrambled onto a bar stool and watched as Cole fixed two mugs of coffee and a glass of chocolate milk, sliding the last one over to her.

"Did we have a sleepover?" she asked.

"I think that would definitely qualify as a sleepover."

"Mommy said I'm not old enough for those yet."

Cole smiled at her from over the rim of his mug. "I think it's fair to say that as long as your mom is with you, it's okay."

"What's okay?" Joy asked, as she hung her coat up and came over to the island.

"Having a sleepover." He deliberately infused his voice with suggestion, and watched as warm color bloomed in Joy's cheeks. He handed her a mug of coffee, amused when she bent her face over the steaming beverage, but not before her eyes promised retribution.

"Are we having breakfast at your house?" Piper asked.

Chocolate milk ringed her upper lip, and Joy reached over to clean her face with a napkin. "Not this morning, sweetie. We should get back to Grammy and Grampy's house. Because you know what today is?"

Piper sat up straight as realization dawned on her face. "Christmas Eve!" She breathed the words reverently.

"That's right, and we have a lot to do to get ready for Santa," Joy said.

Cole watched as Piper gulped down the rest of her milk, and climbed down from the stool, and ran to grab her coat.

"C'mon," she said, looking at them impatiently. "You don't want to miss Santa, do you? He promised this would be the best Christmas ever!"

Cole looked at Joy, but she deliberately avoided eye contact with him, no doubt remembering the one item left on Piper's Christmas list. Looking at Piper, Cole thought he might like to make that Christmas wish come true.

DESPITE THE FACT that Beth had sent an overnight bag over to Cole's house, Joy half expected censure from her and Eldon. But when she and Piper returned to their house, they were greeted with warm hugs and an apple strudel coffee cake straight out of the oven.

Cole followed them into the kitchen, carrying Joy's duffel bag and Piper's gingerbread house.

"Well, look at that!" Beth exclaimed, carefully freeing the house from the cellophane wrapping. "Now that's a delicious-looking gingerbread house! Piper, you did a beautiful job. I just hope nobody eats it before Christmas!"

"Like me," Cole teased, and pretended to steal a gumdrop from the roof, laughing when Beth swatted at his hand. After stealing a piece of coffee cake, instead, he went into the great room to talk with Eldon.

"Did you have fun at Cole's house?" Beth asked Piper, settling the little girl at the kitchen table.

"Yes, we had a sleepover!" she declared.

"How fun," Beth said.

Joy couldn't look at the other woman, and pretended to be absorbed in cutting a slice of coffee cake.

"We decorated Mr. Tanner's tree," Piper continued. She looked at Joy, a question in her eyes. "Can I call him Cole, Mommy?"

Joy flicked a quick glance at Beth. "I think that would be okay, but let's ask him first, okay?"

Beth placed a slice of coffee cake and a glass of orange juice in front of Piper, and then pulled out a chair and sat down with her. "Tell me what you did yesterday. I want to hear about everything!"

Piper launched into an enthusiastic recounting of their day, from milking the pretend cows, to the magical sleigh ride, to decorating the gingerbread tree. Joy wandered into the family room where Eldon and Cole sat watching a football pregame show as they talked about the timber frame business. Lights sparkled on the Christmas tree, and beneath the boughs were piles of gifts, wrapped in paper and tied with ribbons.

"Beth," she said casually, as she returned to the kitchen, "did you know there are Christmas presents under your tree?"

As she'd known would happen, Piper stopped talking in mid-sentence and turned to stare at Joy, before eagerly clambering down to go and see for herself, as Montana bounded behind her. Both women smiled as she squealed in delight, and they heard the deeper voices of the men talking to her.

Beth and Joy smiled at each other.

"It's so wonderful to have a child here for the holidays," Beth said yet again. "We may have to make this our new tradition. Did you enjoy yourself yesterday?"

Joy nodded. "I can't remember the last time I've had so much fun. Cole was a wonderful guide."

"Well, he's a wonderful man," Beth replied. "But I think you already know that."

Joy flushed, wondering just how much the older woman had guessed. "I wanted to ask you something."

Beth removed the tea kettle from where it was whistling on the stove top, and poured the boiling water over her teabag. "I'm listening."

Joy didn't know how to begin, so she took the direct approach. "How would you feel if I told you I'm falling in love with Cole?"

Beth gently stirred her tea, and when she finally looked at Joy, her eyes were moist. She laid her spoon aside, and came around the island to take Joy's hands in her own.

"My darling girl," she said, "Cole is as much my son as Matt ever was. Matt loved you both so much that I believe he would be happy knowing you're together."

Joy nodded, feeling her throat constrict. She had loved Matt with all her heart, and even with the possibility of a new love on the horizon, it was difficult letting that go.

"If you're looking for my blessing," Beth continued, "then you have it."

"Thank you," Joy said. "I just wonder if I'm not rushing into this. Maybe I should go back to California and see how I feel when there's some time and space between us."

"Is that what you want to do?"

"No." She covered her face with her hands and groaned. "I don't know." Lowering her hands, she looked at Beth. "I know you said Cole might quit firefighting and go work for Eldon, and I hope he does. I don't know if my heart can survive another firefighter. If anything were to ever happen to Cole—"

Beth wore an expression of sympathy and understanding. "We can't change the past, my dear, and as you well know, the future isn't guaranteed. You can only control each small moment, which will ultimately determine the direction your life will take." Reaching out, she pulled Joy into a motherly embrace. "You're still young, Joy, and your life is waiting for you. Don't let it get away."

Joy nodded, and pulled back, aware they were both crying a little. Seeing this, they started to laugh, and Joy knew that whatever happened, everything was going to be okay.

Cole chose that moment to walk into the kitchen, and he came to an abrupt stop when he saw them, his brow furrowing with concern.

"What are you two talking about? Are you both *crying?*"

This made the women laugh harder, and Beth reached up to press a kiss against his lean cheek. "We're fine. We were just discussing when—and if—Joy will return to California."

Cole waited until Beth had carried her teacup into the other room, before he turned to Joy. Reaching out, he caught her wrist and tugged her into his arms, his expression still wary.

He tipped her face up with one finger, studying her. "Sure you're okay?"

Joy nodded. Leaning back in his arms, she gave him a tremulous smile. "Yes, I'm sure."

His eyes narrowed, not convinced. "Why are you talking about going back to California?"

"Cole, I need to tell you something. It's important. I—"

Whatever words she had been about to say were interrupted by a knocking on the door. Cole arched an eyebrow. "Hold onto that thought," he said, raising one finger. "We're not done here."

He released her, and Joy leaned against the island, feeling suddenly weak with the realization of what she had almost said to him.

I love you.

Adrenaline kicked in, and she found herself trembling. Was she doing the right thing? She fervently hoped so.

"Can I help you?"

Cole's voice held a note of bewilderment. Curious, Joy crossed the kitchen to peer around his shoulder at the man who stood on the doorstep—a young man dressed in military dress blues, holding a package in his hands. Joy's first thought was that he must be collecting money for a charity. Why else would a uniformed soldier knock on someone's door the day before Christmas?

"Good morning, Sir," the man said crisply. "I'm looking for Eldon Holliday. Is this the correct address?"

Cole stepped back and opened the door wide. "It is, come on in. He's just through here."

The soldier removed his hat and tucked it beneath one arm, carrying the box like a football in his other arm. "I apologize for disturbing your family so close to Christmas, but my superiors decided this couldn't wait," he said, as he followed Cole through the kitchen to the great room.

"Eldon, someone here to see you," Cole announced.

Eldon looked up from where he'd been reading a book to Piper, and his eyebrows shot into his hairline as he saw the visitor. He abruptly stood up, settling Piper back on the sofa.

"Yes?"

Beth stood up too, and both their expressions held such fearful anticipation, that Joy wondered if this was how it had been when they'd received news of Matt's death. Two uniformed forest service officials had come to Joy's house to break the news to her. Had they also sent someone to Glacier Creek? Feeling anxious, she moved to Cole's side, grateful when he slid an arm around her shoulders and pulled her close.

"Sir," the soldier said, speaking directly to Eldon, "I'm Specialist O'Grady. I have been asked to inform you that Harley Ray Tanner has been reported dead in Cheyenne,

Wyoming—"

"*What?*" Abruptly, Cole released Joy and stepped in front of the soldier. "When?"

"Sir, I've been asked to inform Mr. Eldon Holliday that—"

"Harley Ray Tanner is *my father*," Cole interrupted him, his voice harsh. "When did he die?"

For a moment, the soldier looked perplexed, as if his invisible teleprompter had suddenly stopped working. "Sir, I—"

"*When?*"

The soldier flicked a glance between Eldon and Cole. Then he blew out a hard breath, and his rigid shoulders drooped just the tiniest bit.

"Sir," he said, looking at Cole, "On behalf of the Secretary of Defense, I extend to you and your family my deepest sympathy in your great loss. Our records indicate Harley Ray Tanner died on the second day of February, nineteen-ninety-six."

Beth gasped softly. "But that's more than twenty years ago! Why are we only finding out now?"

Specialist O'Grady made a helpless gesture. "This could take some time. Do you mind if I sit down?"

Chapter Fifteen

WHEN THE SOLDIER left an hour later, Cole sat back on the sofa, feeling stunned. *His father had died six weeks after abandoning him in that motel room on Christmas Eve.*

"I suspected he was sick," Eldon said. His eyes had a far-away look as he recalled the days when Harley had worked at the sawmill. "I suggested he see a doctor, but he was stubborn to his very bones. He once said that if something happened to him, you'd go into state care, and that he'd die before he let that happen."

"I guess he was right," Cole said bitterly. "Did you know he was a Vietnam War veteran?"

Eldon shook his head. "He never mentioned it. But if what that army boy said is true, Harley knew his cancer was terminal. That's why he left you behind, knowing we'd take you in."

"Oh, Cole," Joy murmured. She sat beside him on the sofa, and now she hugged him, hard. "I'm so sorry."

Cole accepted her brief embrace, and when she would have released him and stood up, captured her wrist in his hand and tugged her back down beside him. Now, more than ever, he needed her here.

On one level, Cole knew what had happened hadn't been Harley's fault. He'd been sick. But he'd known it, and he'd still left without saying goodbye. Worse, he'd left right after they'd had a huge fight. That alone made his actions unforgivable. He must have known that Cole would blame himself.

"I just can't believe they lost his personal effects after he was admitted to the hospital," Beth said in disbelief.

"Darlin, this is the V.A. we're talking about," Eldon said, and his voice was laced with disgust. "Nothing about that agency surprises me."

The way the soldier had explained it, Harley had made it to a small V.A. clinic just over the Wyoming border, before he'd collapsed and fallen into a coma, suffering from stage four Multiple Myeloma. The symptoms that Beth had mistaken for alcoholism had actually been the symptoms of the disease. The clinic hadn't been equipped to treat him, and had transported him to a larger V.A. hospital in Cheyenne, more than three hundred miles away. During the transfer, Harley had become separated from his personal effects, which had gone into a centralized storage facility. There they had sat for twenty years, until a clerk had been assigned with performing an inventory of the items, and returning them to family members. Only in Harley's case, they hadn't been able to track down any remaining family members, only a former employer—Eldon Holliday.

Now Eldon held the box that Specialist O'Grady had delivered. He looked at Cole, who nodded.

"Open it."

Piper leaned against Cole's knee, watching both him and her grandfather with worried eyes. She didn't understand what was going on, only that the adults were upset. Cole kissed the top of her curly head, trying to provide her with reassurance, but he knew she wasn't buying it.

"Go on, open it," Cole urged again.

Reluctantly, Eldon sliced the tape on the outside of the cardboard box, and opened the flaps. He withdrew a fat, sealed envelope with his name and address on it, and under it the words, *To be Opened by Addressee Only.*

Beneath the envelope were the clothes that Harley had been wearing the day he'd left Glacier Creek, along with his wallet and a small plastic bag containing his military dog tags and a wristwatch. Eldon handed the wallet to Cole. He turned it over in his hands before opening it.

Inside the wallet were forty-three dollars, some photos, Harley's army ID card, and a couple of credit cards. Cole flipped through the plastic sleeves, examining the photos. There were several of him; school photos taken during his kindergarten, first, and second grades. There were several pictures of a pretty blonde woman, posing first with Harley and again with an infant. Pictures of his mother. How many times had he seen his father look at those pictures?

He watched as Eldon carefully opened the envelope. Inside was a folded piece of paper, and yet another sealed envelope. This one had Cole's name scrawled across the front, and Eldon handed it to him, before he unfolded the letter and began to silently read.

As Cole held the envelope in his hands, his heart began

to pound, hard as a sledgehammer against his ribs. He looked at Joy. Her eyes were wide as she watched him, and now she gave him an encouraging smile.

With hands that weren't quite steady, he lifted the flap and withdrew a letter. Tucked inside the letter were two photos, which he glanced at and then handed to Joy. He read the letter once, and then again, before he bent his head into his hands, the paper crumpling in his fingers.

"It's okay, Mr. Tanner." Small hands patted the back of his hands, and Cole looked up to see Piper watching him, her blue eyes clouded with concern. She smiled when he lifted his head, and leaned forward to kiss his cheek. "Don't cry."

Wordlessly, he gathered her into his arms and hugged her tight, breathing in her sweet, innocent, little-girl scent. Maybe she didn't remember the last time she'd seen her own daddy, or even what he looked like, but that didn't mean she didn't miss him as much as Cole had missed his own father.

Kissing the top of her curly head, he released her, and turned to look at Eldon. "You were right. He'd been diagnosed about six months before we came to Glacier Creek. He knew he didn't have much time left, so he wanted to bring me to the one place where my mother had been happiest." He looked at Beth. "To the one person she'd loved like a sister, who he knew would take care of me."

"Your mother?" Beth repeated in bewilderment.

"Here." Joy handed the older woman the photos that Cole had given to her.

Beth took one look at the photos, and drew in a startled

breath as one hand flew to her throat. "Why, this is Laney Dupree!" She raised her gaze to Cole, looking at him as if she'd never seen him before. "She's your mother? I can't believe it!"

Joy looked from Beth to Cole in astonishment. "Your best friend from childhood is Cole's mother?"

"It's why Harley brought Cole here," Eldon said, his voice thick with emotion. He indicated the letter that Harley had left for him. "Laney died when Cole was just a baby, but she'd always talked about growing up in Glacier Creek. So when Harley found out he was sick, he brought Cole here, to us."

Dropping the pictures, Beth stood up and went over to Cole, pulling him to his feet and embracing him. "You've always been a child of my heart. I know Laney would be so proud of the man you've become."

Cole hugged her back, nodding. He had no memory of his mother, but he'd had Beth. She'd treated him like her own child from that first Christmas day, when Eldon had brought him back from the motel room. Eldon stood up and came over, putting his arms around both of them, and laying one hand on the back of Cole's head.

Not to be left out, Piper enthusiastically threw her arms around Cole's legs. Lifting his head, Cole found Joy, and reached out to pull her to her feet and drag her into the group hug.

Piper laughed. "Santa was right! This is going to be the best Christmas ever!"

LATER THAT AFTERNOON, Beth and Eldon took Piper into town for a Christmas choral concert at the local school. Cole and Joy stayed behind, and now they sat curled together on the sofa in front of the fireplace. The fire had long since died down to a glowing bed of coals, but Joy didn't mind. The lights from the Christmas tree cast a soft, twinkling glow across the room, and she was happy just to be with Cole, to lean against his solid frame and have his arm warm around her shoulders. He held her hand in his, and now he laced their fingers together, absently rubbing his thumb across her skin.

"What are you thinking?" she asked, looking at him.

"As much as it bugs me that my dad left that night without saying goodbye, I can finally understand why he did it."

"He knew you wouldn't let him go if he told you he was sick," she said softly. "He knew how much you loved him."

Cole hugged her closer and pressed a kiss against her temple. "I hope so."

"I know so," she said. "He loved you. That's why he brought you here, to Glacier Creek. To give you the best possible chance for a loving home and a happy childhood after he was gone. Eldon said it; he was afraid you'd go into foster care if something happened to him."

Cole was silent for several minutes. "I did have a loving home. Beth and Eldon took me in and treated me like a second son. I think some of the guilt I've carried all these years isn't related to the argument we had before my father left, but my own relief that he didn't make me go with him."

"Don't feel guilty about not wanting to go back on the road with him," Joy said earnestly. "You were just a little boy, and for the first time in a long time, you had a stable life and people around you who made you feel welcome and loved. That's what your father wanted for you. You had no idea he was sick. I wouldn't be surprised if he actually instigated the argument you two had that night, just to make it easier for you to let him go."

Cole gave a huff of laughter. "That sounds like something he might do."

"I'm sure he wouldn't want you to feel guilty," Joy said. "He would want you to be happy, and to live your life joyfully."

Raising her hand to his mouth, Cole pressed a kiss against her a palm. "That should be easy, now that I have you in my life. Which reminds me, we were having an interesting discussion before the army invaded."

Joy flushed, recalling exactly what she'd been about to tell him before the solider had arrived. "What were we talking about?" she asked, feigning ignorance.

Cole drew in a deep breath, and then shifted on the sofa to face her, taking both her hands in his. "I was hoping you might want to come out here, to Montana."

Joy stared at him, hope and disbelief warring within her. Her heart began to race in her chest. "What are you saying, Cole?"

His expression was so intense that her breath caught.

"I know we haven't known each other very long, but I

am falling in love with you, Joy Holliday." He drew in a deep breath. "I'm just asking you to give us a chance to figure this thing out, and it would be a whole lot easier if you didn't live a thousand miles away."

"Are you asking me to move here, to Glacier Creek?"

Cole looked down at their joined hands for a moment, and when he looked back at her, she could see the stark vulnerability in his eyes. "When I heard you were coming here for Christmas, I wanted to dislike you," he confessed. "I already resented you for being the reason Matt moved away."

Joy stared at him in disbelief. "You disliked me?"

Cole half-laughed, and shook his head. "No, sweetheart. From the first second I laid eyes on you, I was toast. I *wanted* to dislike you, and instead I found myself understanding why Matt left Montana. Which is why, if you don't want to come out here, I'll come out to California."

"Oh, Cole..." She didn't know what to say, so instead she leaned in and kissed him, hoping the kiss would convey all the pent-up emotions she felt.

Cole groaned and set her a little away from him. "I want so badly to carry you up those stairs to your bedroom, but I need to know if there's a chance for us."

Her heart knew she needed to grab this man with both hands and never let him go. But her head was more stubborn. "Cole, I want to be with you. Earlier today, in the kitchen, I was going to tell you that I've fallen in love with you, too. And I know Piper loves you. But..." She gave him a shaky smile. "You're a wildland firefighter. What if something happened to you? I don't think I could survive that."

"Hang on a sec," he said, standing up. "Don't go any-where."

He disappeared into the kitchen, while Joy sat on the sofa and waited. She rubbed her hands on the tops of her thighs and drew in a deep, steadying breath. When he came back he had a small, wrapped gift box in his hand.

"I was going to give this to you tomorrow morning," he said, sitting close to her, "but I think now is the right time."

He handed the box to her. Joy moistened her suddenly dry lips. The box looked suspiciously like a jeweler's box, but surely he wouldn't—

She jerked her gaze up to his. "What is it?"

"Just open it."

Joy did, pulling the bright red paper and silver ribbon off, and carefully opening the box. Inside, nestled on a bed of deep red velvet, lay a beautiful Cloisonné hummingbird. With a soft gasp of delight, Joy lifted it from the box by a slender gold ribbon. It was an ornament, richly enameled in deep reds, greens, and blues, and accented in gold. The bird's long delicate beak was cast in gold, and its eyes were match-ing sapphires. The gleaming enamel and the gems caught the light from the tree, and sparkled in her hand.

"How beautiful" she breathed.

Cole pulled her to her feet, and they walked over to the Christmas tree to hang the little bird on one of the branches.

"This one will never shatter, never hurt you," he said, sliding his arms around her. "I promise."

"How did you—"

"Sweetheart, if the hummingbirds you see are trying to

send us a message, I'm not about to ignore them." He cupped her face in his big hands, his eyes searching hers. "I haven't celebrated Christmas in a long time, but you and Piper are my Christmas miracle. You've made me believe in magic again."

"Oh, Cole…"

"Will you stay?"

She slanted him a shy smile. "That depends on your intentions."

Cole laughed softly and kissed her. "Where you're concerned, my intentions are always wicked." Then he grew serious. "I thought I'd start by building a room where you can work on your pottery. You already have a client here in town, and I know your business is going to be as successful here as it is in California. If you're not comfortable moving in with me right away, then I know Eldon and Beth would love to have you stay here. Then, after a brief but whirlwind courtship, we'll get married and live happily ever after."

"Mmm," she said thoughtfully. "That does sound pretty appealing. But what about your job?"

"I've been giving that some serious thought," he said. "I'd like to stay involved with the local firefighters on a volunteer basis," he said, "but I'd no longer be part of the smokejumper crew, and I'd no longer be battling wildfires around the country."

Joy looked sharply at him, unwilling to believe he could so easily give up such a big part of his life. "But you love what you do with the smokejumpers. I don't want you to quit because of me. Eventually, you might *really* come to resent me."

"I wouldn't be leaving the jump crew because of you." He thought for a moment. "At least, not entirely. It's something I've been considering doing for a while now. Fighting wildfires was always Matt's dream, and I was happy to go along for the ride. But after he died, so did the excitement of being a smokejumper."

"Yes," Joy said. "Battling wildfires was in his blood, and he lived for the next big blaze. His enthusiasm for the job was contagious. As long as you're leaving for your own reasons, and not because of me, I can definitely live with that."

Joy leaned her forehead against Cole's chest, overcome with relief to know that he wouldn't continue jumping out of planes to battle wildfires. She'd already given her heart to Cole, but the knowledge she wouldn't have to watch him leave for work, not knowing if he would return, was the best Christmas gift of all.

"Will you take Eldon up on his offer?" she asked.

Cole looked down at her with an expression of surprise. "You know about that?"

Joy laughed. "You did mention it, but Beth told me about it, and how Eldon would like to retire."

"Yes. Eldon approached me several months ago and asked if I'd consider taking over the timber frame business. He'd continue to act as a consultant, but I'd become the new CEO." He paused. "It would be a full time job."

"Is it what you want?"

"I've been working the sawmill and raising frames since I

was a teenager," Cole replied. "I had a good mentor in Eldon, and I enjoy the work, both the designing and the building."

"If your own house is any indication, you're going to be very successful," Joy said.

"What about you?" he asked.

"What about me?"

"Do you think you could relocate to Glacier Creek? I know you have a life in Santa Barbara, with family and a business and an established clientele. You'd be giving up a lot to come out here."

"I'd be giving up even more if I didn't," she responded. "But I think I could make it work. I could hire one of my master students full-time to run the studio and continue training new students on how to throw the pieces and glaze the green ware." She smiled at him. "We would need to go out to Santa Barbara every three or four months to check on the business and visit my parents, but I think that's doable, don't you? It would be wonderful to have a studio here in Montana and one on the West Coast."

"I've always liked Santa Barbara," Cole said with a smile.

Joy's eyes drifted closed as he covered her mouth with his. The kiss started out tender, and then turned hot. Gathering her closer, Cole deepened the kiss, angling her face for better access. Joy hummed with pleasure as she threaded her fingers through his thick hair, knowing she'd found her own Christmas miracle.

Chapter Sixteen

CHRISTMAS MORNING DAWNED bright and clear, and Cole arrived early, bringing Lucy and her one remaining puppy with him. He carried the little dog into the kitchen under his arm, and Piper laughed in delight when she saw the big red bow around its neck. Eldon seemed genuinely moved when Cole handed the puppy to him.

"What are you going to call her?" Piper asked.

"Well, I don't know," Eldon said, rubbing under the puppy's chin. "You and I will have to think of something."

Cole rubbed his hands together in anticipation and looked at Piper with a twinkle in his eyes. "When do we get to open presents?"

Piper, still in her pajamas, jumped up and down in excitement. "Now! Grammy and Grampy said we had to wait for you to get here."

"I think we can move into the other room," Beth said, smiling. She picked up a tray laden with pastries, orange juice, and coffee. "I'll just set this on the coffee table."

"I already opened my Christmas stocking," Piper told Cole, and then dropped her voice to a conspiratorial whisper. "But there's one for you, too! Come see!"

Laughing, Cole allowed himself to be pulled into the family room, where a fire crackled in the fireplace, and four stockings, filled to overflowing, hung from the mantle. The Christmas tree sparkled in the corner of the room, and beneath the boughs were piled dozens of wrapped gifts.

Eldon took the heavy tray from Beth, exchanging a warm kiss with her before he carried the tray into the other room and placed it on the large coffee table. Joy followed, and then stood for a moment taking in the scene. Under Piper's direction, Cole took down each stocking, handing one to Beth and another to Eldon. That was when Joy noticed that something had changed.

Above the stockings, on the mantle itself, were a series of framed pictures. There was the photo of Laney Dupree holding her infant son, Cole, and another photo of Laney and Harley together. A third photo showed Cole and Matt as young boys, their arms flung around each other's shoulders as they laughed into the camera. Next to that was a photo of Joy, several photos of Piper, and two more of Matt as a child. The photos of father and daughter, taken at about the same age, were almost identical. Joy's heart hitched as she looked at each of them.

Beth came to stand beside her, linking her arm through Joy's. "The photos were Eldon's idea. He said we should have pictures of our family on the mantle. Our entire family."

"They're perfect," Joy said through a sheen of tears.

As Cole took down Joy's stocking, he turned to look for her, and their eyes met. Joy's heart turned over at the expression of love in Cole's eyes as he smiled at her across the room.

Walking over to him, she accepted the stocking, and then leaned up and pressed a kiss against his mouth, infusing all the love and hope she felt into the action.

"Mommy!" Piper exclaimed. "You're kissing Mr. Tanner!"

Laughing, they broke apart and moved to sit side by side on the sofa with their stockings across their laps. Piper sat close to Joy.

"Do you two love each other?" she asked, her expression curious.

"We do," Joy said, looking at Cole.

"Is that okay?" Cole asked.

Piper eyed him cautiously. "Does this mean we get to stay in Glacier Creek?"

"I think that can be arranged," Joy confirmed, laughing.

"Yes!" Piper flung her arms around her mother, hugging her tightly. "Santa was right! Everything I wished for came true!"

Montana barked in excitement, and the second puppy leaped on him, until the two dogs were rolling on the floor, growling as they played.

Eldon laughed at their antics, before leaning forward to slap Cole on the back. His voice was gruff with emotion. "Well, that's fine news, son. Just fine."

"The best news," Beth said, beaming.

"Open your stockings!" Piper insisted, and then dramatically flung up her arms. "I've been waiting *forever*."

Something glittered in the corner of the room, and Joy looked to see that a beam of sunlight had caught the sapphires on the hummingbird ornament, causing them to sparkle. Lacing her fingers with Cole's, she drew his attention to the ornament. As they admired the effect, a movement outside the window caught Joy's attention.

On the other side of the glass hovered a tiny hummingbird, a real one that seemed to look in at them. As Joy and Cole watched in awe, it hovered for a moment longer, before flitting away and soaring upwards, into the heavens.

The End

MONTANA
BORN

Christmas has hit Montana Born! Check out these other holiday stories.

A Baby for Christmas by Joan Kilby

Their Christmas Carol by Jessica Gilmore

His Christmas Bride by Lara Van Hulzen

Christmas at the Graff by Kaylie Newell

A Little Christmas Magic by Barbara Ankrum

Their Christmas Miracle by Lynne Marshall

A Crazy Little Christmas by Megan Crane

Miracle on Chance Avenue by Jane Porter

Available now at your favorite online retailer!

About the Author

Karen Foley admits to being an incurable romantic. When she's not working for the Department of Defense, she loves writing sexy stories about alpha heroes and strong heroines. Karen lives in New England with her husband, two daughters, and a houseful of pets.

Thank you for reading

A Hummingbird Christmas

If you enjoyed this book, you can find more from all our great authors at TulePublishing.com, or from your favorite online retailer.

TULE
PUBLISHING